SO-CWT-884

WITHDRAWN

The White Pony

THE
WHITE
PONY

by Mary Oldham

Apollo Memorial Library

HASTINGS HOUSE, PUBLISHERS

New York, N.Y. 10016

Copyright © 1981 by Mary Oldham

All rights reserved. No part of this publication may be
reproduced, stored in a retrieval system, or transmitted,
in any form or by any means, electronic, mechanical,
photocopying, recording or otherwise, without the prior
permission of the copyright owner or the publishers.

Library of Congress Cataloging in Publication Data

Oldham, Mary.   The white pony.
  Summary: An overweight girl becomes attached to a
nearly blind white pony who inspires her to develop her
writing talent and to tackle her biggest problem as
well.
  [1. Weight control—Fiction.   2. Ponies—Fiction.
3. Authorship—Fiction]   I. Title.
PZ7.0454Wh   1981   [Fic]   81-4135
ISBN 0-8038-0800-3

Printed in the United States of America

Contents

CHAPTER ONE

Mount Severn

PEGGY LINDSAY sat on a stool outside the back door at Mount Severn Stables, a sketch pad balanced on her knee. She was making pencil drawings of Bianca, the white pony who wandered hesitantly about the sun-baked yard, touching and sniffing the stable door, the dog-cart, the water trough.

"I bet you she won't like horses," Peggy said.

"Oh, don't be so grumpy," said her mother, through the open kitchen window.

"It'll be all high heels and make-up, I know these townies," said Peggy. "Think they're so sophisticated."

"You'd be at the lipstick yourself, given half a chance," said her mother.

There was no arguing with grownups, thought Peggy. As if having somebody you didn't know living with you would be the easiest thing on earth. It was just like her mother to land them with this. Oh yes, she had told the new teacher, the flat will be vacant after August. You simply must stay with us while you look for a house. And you have a daughter Peggy's age too? How nice, they're sure to get on together.

"They're here, they're here!" Tessa and Ian, Peggy's younger brother and sister, came rushing round from the garden. The sound of a car was heard, changing gear to turn into the short steep lane leading to Mount Severn. A

moment later a green Volkswagen drove into the yard
and drew to a halt.

"Someone catch Bianca, for goodness' sake," called
Peggy's mother, hastening out of the kitchen towards the
car. "Ian, go and fetch your father and Sybille."

Ian ran off while Peggy and Tessa lurked behind
Bianca to take a first look at the new arrivals. The grownups were standing by the car and the woman had turned
to pull the front seat forward to let the third person get
out.

The daughter of my age, thought Peggy. She stared
across the yard in disappointment and annoyance at the
girl who waited shyly while Peggy's mother introduced
herself. The girl had light auburn hair in plaits, and a
very pink face. She wore a loose brown cotton shirt and
grey trousers which did not disguise the fact that she was
very fat.

How awful, thought Peggy. She's enormous.

Then the girl caught sight of Bianca and her face lit
up. She blushed as she realized she was being observed,
but her pleased expression remained.

She does like horses after all, thought Peggy, but what
an awful creep.

Peggy's mother beckoned her and Tessa over with a
steely "manners-or-else" look. "Peggy, Tessa, come and
meet Mr. and Mrs. Dawes and Barbara." Tessa danced
forward with a toothy smile; Peggy followed more slowly.
She shook Barbara's hand self-consciously. It was plump
and hot.

Barbara Dawes smiled uncertainly at Peggy and Mrs.
Lindsay. Peggy's mother had a very friendly, freckled
face and short, curly hair, even redder than Barbara's
own. Peggy looked more formidable, brown and frown-

ing. Barbara had not missed Peggy's registering how fat she was. She won't want me anywhere near her pony, thought Barbara, not moving from her father's side.

Screwing up her eyes against the sun, Barbara looked around the yard. Oh dear, but what a lovely place, she thought. It was obviously a stableyard, shaded on the south by the large red brick house with its steep roof and many gables. There were silvery, wooden barns, a water trough, a haystack, and horse shoes nailed on the stable doors. A wide gate opened onto paddocks which rose steeply up a long hill. In the nearest, flattest one, ponies and riders trotted lethargically in a circle while a small person on a tall brown horse called out commands and corrections.

"It's a lovely old house, but far too big, of course," Mrs. Lindsay was saying to Barbara's parents. She turned as some more people arrived from the garden. "Here's Ian, my middle child, and my husband, David." Mr. Lindsay shook hands all around and gave Barbara a warm smile.

But Barbara scarcely noticed Peggy's father. She stared instead at the woman who had come strolling round with him. She looked about the same age as Peggy's mother. She had a vibrant, suntanned face and a tumbling mass of curly dark hair. She wore a bright patchwork skirt which fell nearly to the ground and swung out as she walked. In proportion to her height she was easily as fat as Barbara, and she looked as though she didn't give two hoots. She grinned at the children.

"This is Sybille Jones, who's about to leave us for her own place," said Mrs. Lindsay.

Peggy smiled smugly. People were always impressed when they met Sybille. "She teaches French," Peggy told Barbara. "She's ever so strict at school, but she's super

fun at home." She looked cautiously at Barbara. "What
do your Mum and Dad teach?"

"Uh, my father teaches math," Barbara said. "And my
mother's going to be the school librarian." Barbara could
not take her eyes off Sybille. She was fat—but *beautiful*.

"Do come in and see the flat," Sybille was saying, shaking hands with Barbara's parents.

"Perhaps Barbara would like to meet Bianca," Mrs.
Lindsay gestured across the yard at the white pony.
"She's very gentle."

Barbara looked at her mother who caught her eye with
a rather amused, rueful glance.

"I didn't realize you ran a riding school," Mrs. Dawes
said, taking her husband's arm and moving off towards
the house.

"Well, sort of," Mrs. Lindsay answered. "We do a bit of
everything really, teach riding, break in ponies for people. . ."

Barbara went shyly over to stroke the white pony who
sighed and stretched her neck out for more, her eyelids
with their thick white lashes blinking dreamily.

"Her name's Bianca," said Tessa informatively at her
side. "But she's no good, she's blind. We don't ride her,
we're going to breed from her."

"Be quiet, Tessa," said Peggy sharply. "You're telling
lies anyway." She leaned across Bianca's withers and
stroked a downy shoulder. "She's not blind, she's only
very short-sighted. And she's too young to ride yet. Anyway, it doesn't matter because she's our beautiful Bianca,
she's our mascot, aren't you, Love?"

"She should have been a palomino, but she came out
wrong." said Ian. "What did Miss Brown say she was
called?"

"A blue-eyed cream," said Peggy. "That's what you

sometimes get if you breed from two palominos. The owner wanted to have her put down, but Miss Brown said she'd buy her."

Barbara smiled and nodded. "Saved from slaughter," she said softly, stroking Bianca's nose with the back of her stubby forefinger. "She's lovely," Barbara murmured. "Just like a white palfrey. Like the great medieval ladies used to ride. You know, with jewelled velvet saddles and a liveried page to stand at the bridle."

Peggy was startled and impressed by this description of Bianca. Barbara could not be as hopeless as she looked. She began to feel guilty for assuming that because Barbara was fat she must be boring and useless. She could imagine what Sybille would say about such ideas.

Peggy smiled grudgingly at Barbara. "Do you like horses?"

Barbara grinned self-consciously. "I'm afraid I really love horses," she said, still gently stroking Bianca. "I can hardly believe I might be living next to a riding school. It's too good to be true."

"Oh good, then you can help too. We all muck in."

"We all muck in to muck out," Ian chuckled, joyfully repeating an old joke.

Peggy explained to Barbara. "It means clean up, you know, the stalls, the equipment . . ."

"Ugh, I hate mucking out!" Tessa said. "And cleaning tack. When I'm a famous show-jumper I shall have a groom to do all the boring jobs." she told Barbara. "I'm going to be a show-jumper and ride for Wales in the Olympic Games just like—" her excited voice was drowned in Peggy and Ian's loud groans.

Just then Mr. Dawes appeared at the kitchen door. "Come on if you want to see the flat, Barbara," he called.

Barbara gave Bianca a reluctant last pat and they all

trooped into the house through a wide hall with a black and white tiled floor.

"Come and see our bedrooms, they're much the nicest," said Peggy to Barbara. "You can look at the flat after." She bounded upstairs ahead of the grownups. Barbara panted obediently after Peggy. The house seemed endlessly huge, with corridors and staircases leading round unexpected corners.

Several flights later, Peggy and Barbara reached the very top floor where the Lindsay children each had a tiny bedroom with a gabled window. In Peggy's room there were several shelves of books which Barbara, having gotten her breath back, squatted on the floor to examine. Among the collections of fairy tales and classics like *Little Women* was a whole shelf of very old books which turned out to be the horse stories of twenty-five years before. They all had "Nancy Evans" written childishly on the flyleaf.

"Those old ones were Mum's when she was a little girl," said Peggy.

Barbara looked up at her in wonder. "Your mother was Nancy Evans?"

"Yup." Peggy always enjoyed people's reactions when they realized who her mother was.

Barbara paused. "*The* Nancy Evans?"

Peggy nodded.

"The Nancy Evans who was the youngest person ever to win an Olympic medal for horse-jumping?"

Peggy nodded again and flopped on her quilt-covered bed. Barbara turned back to the bookshelves. She looked at the collection with awe.

"I expect you read quite a lot, don't you, with your mother a librarian?" Peggy smiled nonchalantly.

"Yes." Barbara answered slowly, trying to collect her thoughts. "But she thinks I read too many horse books. She doesn't approve of them. She says they encourage too much competitiveness or something." Barbara gently turned a small dog-eared volume in her hands. "She doesn't usually buy too many horse stories for the library."

"Crumbs," said Peggy. "That won't go down very well at school. Nobody reads anything except horse books."

"Sounds like quite a civilized place," said Barbara, and they both giggled.

The sound of hooves floated up from the yard. 'That's the end of the riding class," said Peggy, jumping to her feet. "Let's go and help Miss Brown with the ponies."

They hurried downstairs. The Lindsays had left it to Sybille to show Barbara's mother and father around the flat and were preparing tea in the kitchen. Barbara was pleased to see a fruit loaf and homemade biscuits cooling on a cake rack. She caught Mr. Lindsay's eye and he winked. He was a small dark person with a lot of silky hair and a large nose. He wore loose corduroy trousers and a collarless shirt. Barbara was very much struck by the fact that Mr. Lindsay was shorter than his wife, and hardly taller than Barbara herself. She smiled shyly in return and followed Peggy outside.

The yard was full of ponies. Children were dismounting, loosening girths and feeding tidbits. Peggy led Barbara into a long dark stable where a slight figure was unsaddling a very lovely dark brown horse. Bianca followed and sniffed at the new arrivals. The dark brown horse bent to greet her with a low whinny.

Barbara saw another very small person, with thin white hair, wrinkled brown skin, eyes as blue as Bianca's and absurdly large teeth. She wore a white shirt and jodhpurs which made her look curiously schoolgirlish.

"Miss Brown, this is Barbara," Peggy said. "Her mother and father are looking at Sybille's flat."

"It's very nice to meet you, my dear," Miss Brown said quietly. She had a sweet smile and a very strong Welsh accent.

Peggy was patting the brown horse. "Hello Consy, have you been good?"

"That isn't Coningsby? The horse that won the medal?" said Barbara in astonishment.

"Why yes," Miss Brown smiled. "He doesn't look too bad for a retired gentleman of twenty-eight, does he?"

Barbara's eyes sparkled; she shook her head.

"He's going a bit grey now, like me," said Miss Brown. She rubbed Coningsby's nose affectionately and he snorted at her.

Barbara reached out to stroke the still glossy neck. "I can't believe it," she said. "I saw a film of him jumping in the Olympics all that time ago. It doesn't seem possible that I'm here touching the very same horse."

Miss Brown laughed softly and went off to supervise the unsaddling. Barbara lingered to gaze at the two horses in the dim light. There was something mysterious and magical about them, the aged, but still elegant thoroughbred and the fey insubstantial white pony: like horses in a legend, thought Barbara. You felt that they might almost grow wings, or speak to you. She stretched out her fingers shyly to the pony touching the pink muzzle. Bianca blew down her nostrils, tickling Barbara's palm.

"She likes you," said Peggy. "You're quiet with her. It makes her jump when people come upon her suddenly with loud noises."

"She's lovely," said Barbara, moved. *She likes you . . .* perhaps this was the pony, *the* pony . . . A picture slid into Barbara's mind of herself, marvellously slim and athletic, sitting tight on a small white horse as it flew recklessly over enormous fences, to deafening roars of applause from the crowd.

"You're quite used to horses, aren't you?" said Peggy, watching Barbara fondle Bianca. "Can you ride?"

"Sort of," said Barbara, flushing, "but I'm not very good." She didn't want to think about the humiliation that had attended most of her attempts.

"I like trekking best, you just amble along looking at the view," said Peggy. "And you can have a canter if you want it. I'm not much of a one for horse shows, I'll leave them to Tessa any time."

"Oh, hear hear," agreed Barbara, although the small white horse still leapt fences in her mind.

Tea was laid in the large and faded living room. The younger children had already piled their plates high and were crouching on the floor in a corner in front of a small television.

"Help yourselves to anything you like, no formality today." said Mrs. Lindsay to Barbara and Peggy.

Barbara looked hungrily at the laden table, trying to avoid her mother's warning eye. But Mrs. Dawes said, "Don't go mad, Barbara." She spoke quietly but her warning fell clearly into a lull in the conservation. Everyone looked at Barbara, who flushed guiltily.

"She loves her food, don't you, Ba," said her father kindly.

Sybille laughed. "I know the feeling," she said. "Pass us that *bara brith*, Peggy." *Bara brith* was the fruit loaf, sliced and buttered. It looked delicious. Barbara loved dark and fruity food. She shot a grateful glance at Sybille and received an amused wink in return.

Miss Brown came shyly into the room just then and was introduced all round, enabling Barbara to position herself near enough to the table to eat freely and unobtrusively. Peggy ate heartily too, yet she was as thin as anything, Barbara noted, reflecting for the thousandth time on the injustice of it all.

Miss Brown was saying, "And so they like the flat?" She addressed Mrs. Lindsay but was smiling at the Daweses.

"It's a lovely flat," said Barbara's father. "I haven't seen a view like the one from that front window for years."

"It *is* lovely," agreed Barbara's mother. "There's plenty of space too."

"That's settled then," said Mrs. Lindsay. "Unless you'd prefer to think things over for a day or two."

Oh no, thought Barbara, swallowing a mouthful of cake far too quickly, I'll die if I don't know for certain *now*.

But her mother said, "Goodness, if you're happy to have us we'll be very happy to come. Don't you think, Mike? Barbara?"

Barbara was overwhelmed with relief. She forgave her mother the remark about the food. She said, "Oh *yes*," in a rush, and reddened yet again as everyone laughed.

"Oh dear, I hope we've done the right thing," Barbara's mother said in the car on the way home. "Perhaps we should have thought it over for a day or two after all. It's such a big step, moving in with a completely strange family."

"Now don't start worrying yourself," said Barbara's father, patting his wife reassuringly on the knee. "It'll be only for a while. And look how welcoming they were. You said so yourself."

"I suppose so," said Barbara's mother. "I hope they're not too overwhelming though. They're not what you'd expect Welsh schoolteachers to be like, are they? That Sybille would be more at home in a public bar. Did you see her bathroom? Silver wallpaper!" She turned around and caught Barbara's dreamy expression. "Don't think you'll be able to hang around those stables all day long, Barbara," she said. "They won't be giving away any free rides, you know."

"Peggy said I could help," said Barbara, her daydreams of riding Bianca gaily over the Welsh hills shrivelling inside her.

"I daresay Peggy did. But it'll be what Miss Brown says that counts, or more likely what Mrs. Lindsay says."

"Leave her alone, Joan," said Barbara's father mildly. "She won't get in the way, will you Barbara? And I should think we'll be able to find the money to let you have a ride now and again."

"Gosh, thanks, Dad."

"You'd better try to lose a bit of that weight, then," said her mother.

Barbara glared at her mother's back.

CHAPTER TWO

Resolutions and Secrets

BARBARA poured cereal into a bowl, and looked into the box to make sure that the level hadn't dropped enough for her mother to notice. She added milk and a large spoonful of sugar, and ate standing up by the kitchen table.

She might have known that her mother and father wouldn't go off for the day and leave her alone with a larder full of food to steal. Cereal was about all there was, apart from boring diet foods like melba toast and fruit.

But it didn't matter today. She had been saving her pocket money for just this occasion.

As soon as she was sure her parents were safely on the London train she let herself out of the house, shopping basket in hand, and spent quite a while wandering back and forth between the grocery and the bakery. It was no small problem to decide what to buy, to stretch her money to include as many of her favorite foods as possible. Especially because today, Barbara vowed, was to be her last great feast.

Her mother had left hamburgers and salad and fruit yogurt in the refrigerator for Barbara's lunch. These would do for later. Barbara hated salad anyway, it was so cold. For the feast, Barbara finally decided on some sticky, fruity buns, some bananas, a cream doughnut and a package of chocolate biscuits. The lady in the bakery gave Barbara an amused look as she handed over the box of cakes, and Barbara walked home pink in the face thinking up cutting remarks she could have made.

At home, she carried the food, still in its boxes and paper bags, up to her bedroom. Somehow she could not bring herself to lay it all out on plates. That way she would have to look at it all at once. If she left the food in its wrappings it would be more secret. Part of her was aghast at the thought of so many buns and biscuits. "But you've got to eat it all, it's your last great feast," she told herself, biting into the cream doughnut.

When the feast was eaten, the final few chocolate biscuits washed down with a large mug of sweet, milky coffee, Barbara was left with the familiar sickish, overfull bloatedness that made resolutions about last great feasts very easy.

I need never have this horrible sick feeling again, she told herself as she had done so often before. But this time things were different. She wouldn't need to have any more secret feasts now that her private dream world was about to become a reality: the countryside; a riding school; an Olympic medal winning rider *and* horse *and* trainer; a colorful, witty and intelligent family for neighbors; and the pony, above all, the white pony.

The memory of that quiet moment in the stable, Bianca's blowing softly at her hand, Peggy's saying, "She likes you", haunted Barbara. She relived it fifty times a day. It formed the opening scene of the story she was now writing, which was about a pony exactly like Bianca, short sight and all. A family rather like the Lindsays came into it too.

Barbara creaked to her feet (ugh! she was full) and found the thick notebook in which she was writing the story. She had reached an exciting part—a gypsy had hinted of a secret herbal cure for the pony's eyesight. But he wanted a lot of money for the secret, more than the heroine could afford. Barbara had gotten stuck here for a way to get the gypsy to change his mind. She dismissed the idea of having the heroine save the gypsy's baby son from drowning.

Despite this problem it was marvellous how the story was coming along. It was much better than either of the other two she had written, much more true to life. Her mother wouldn't have thought so of course; she believed all horse stories were rubbish.

Barbara drew tiny horses round the margins of the page in front of her. I need a bit more inspiration, she thought. I'll be seeing Bianca again soon, she'll inspire me. Barbara began to daydream about her new life in Wales. She tore off a clean sheet of paper from the back of her notebook and wrote at the top: "Resolutions for when I'm in Wales."

The first one was: "Finish 'The Blind Pony.'" This was the title of the new story. Barbara knew what the ending would be. The heroine—who was amazingly like Barbara (but not fat)—would defy all who said the blind pony was useless because of her eyesight, and ride her to victory at the Horse of the Year Show. There would be a breathtaking finale as the jumps rose higher and higher, and a great gasp from the huge audience as the white pony cleared the final wall . . .

Next Barbara wrote resolutely: "No more secret feasts."

It would not be easy. Her new bedroom at Mount Severn was a wonderfully private place with lots of dark corners under the sloping ceiling, and a little gabled window looking out onto the Bryn Bank. It was just the place to curl up with a fire and a book and a box of biscuits on a dark winter's evening with the wind and the rain rattling around the chimney. Perhaps the room and the atmosphere would make up for the biscuits. Barbara envisioned the room painted in rich interesting colors, with crocheted patchwork blankets thrown over the bed and the chairs. Perhaps I could crochet a blanket, thought Barbara vaguely.

Next she wrote: "Learn to ride really well and get a pony," with several exclamation marks because for the first time this seemed to have some chance of coming true. Despite her mother's dampening remarks, Barbara sensed that Peggy had been perfectly sincere when she had told her she could help with the ponies; Barbara had the impression that at Mount Severn, everyone helped with whatever needed doing. It would be wonderful to be accepted as part of the riding school crowd, a status she had never achieved at the stables near her present home. Barbara was filled with the sensation that her real life with horses was just beginning, and anything could happen. Perhaps she really would be able to learn to ride well despite her weight; perhaps she might even one day share a glorious destiny with Bianca. Barbara jumped to her feet in excitement, her imagination running away with her.

Her parents had left a supply of empty cardboard boxes in her room. She was supposed to be packing her things, not sitting and eating and writing stories and daydreaming. At least today she could pack everything she wanted to take without her mother watching her. Barbara wrapped up her precious stories (the first two were neatly copied into fresh, stiff-backed notebooks, the third, unfinished one was still in its untidy pencil scrawl, full of alterations and doodles) and hid them in the largest carton under some old horsy magazines.

The carton was topped with books, of which Barbara possessed a large number. She took the precaution of not packing all the pony books in one box, in case her mother discovered which one it was and contrived to get it accidentally lost or destroyed in the move. Barbara did not really believe her mother would do such a thing but, she told herself darkly, you never know.

She tied up the cartons with a good deal of nylon string and tested their weight. When I open them again it will mean the beginning of a totally new life, she thought. A life with horses. A life with Bianca.

"Where's Bianca?"

Less than a week later Barbara stood in the stable yard at Mount Severn looking about her. There was tremendous noise and confusion as the moving men began to unload the furniture and packing cases.

"She's in the stable," said Peggy. "She's hurt herself."

"Hurt herself!" said Barbara, staring at Peggy with horror. "What happened? Is she all right?"

"She stood on some glass," Peggy started for the stable. "Come and see."

"Lend a hand, Barbara," her mother called. "Here's the ironing board, you can carry that up." Mrs. Dawes looked flustered.

"Two minutes, Mother, please," begged Barbara. "I must go and see if Bianca's all right."

Barbara's mother groaned, but fairly good-humoredly. "I might have known. All right, two minutes."

Bianca stood in the stable, resting a foreleg. She jerked her head up and whinnied as the two girls approached. Barbara had forgotten what a strange, luminous coat Bianca had, and what large sad eyes.

"Good girl, good girl," said Peggy. "Let's just have a look at you."

"Hello, Bianca," said Barbara softly, stroking the pony's nose.

Peggy climbed over the partition and bent to pick up Bianca's hoof. "Look, there's the scar . . . it's healing pretty well." Barbara saw a dark, dried-up gash at the back edge of the pony's hoof cupped in Peggy's hand.

"Some beast threw a beer bottle into the paddock and it broke." Peggy lowered the hoof gently and patted Bianca.

"Poor, poor pony," Barbara murmured in Bianca's ear, thinking that she must bring the incident into her story somehow.

"She was so frightened, poor little thing. But the vet gave her a tetanus shot and things, so it's just a matter of time, Mum says."

Barbara looked sadly at the injured pony. "I've got some sugar lumps," she said. "Is it all right for me to give her one? I know they're supposed to be bad for her teeth."

"Well, now and again doesn't hurt," said Peggy. She picked up Bianca's water bucket and peered into it. "She needs some more water."

"Oh, I'll get it," said Barbara quickly.

"Okay," Peggy said. She climbed back over the partition and dropped the bucket at Barbara's feet. "You've really fallen for Bianca, haven't you?" she smiled.

"She's so lovely." Barbara blushed. She held out two sugar lumps on her palm and Bianca took them between her lips, crunching them and nodding her head. Barbara picked up the water bucket and took it outside to fill it at the trough. Peggy went to help the moving men who were maneuvering beds into the house, shouting instructions at one another.

The bucket of water was heavy. Barbara heaved it slowly over the partition and lowered it onto Bianca's thick bedding of wood shavings and straw. Then she climbed awkwardly over the partition and slipped the bucket into a bracket in the wall. Now Bianca couldn't kick it over. As Barbara set it carefully into place she felt a soft muzzle at her ear, and there was Bianca directly behind her.

"You only want more sugar, don't you?" she said to Bianca. But she was filled with happiness. She knows me, she thought. She likes me. I'm right in the corner of the stable behind her but I don't feel a bit scared. I know she'll never bite me or kick me. And she came right across to me, even with her sore foot.

"Two minutes, I said," Barbara's mother called from the stable door.

"Oh . . . okay . . . sorry," said Barbara reluctantly. She gave Bianca two more lumps of sugar, and eased herself out of the corner. Bianca's eyes were dark and shadowed in the dim light of the stable, but Barbara felt sure that the pony watched her as she clambered back over the partition.

"I'll be back later," she told her.

Peggy, Tessa and Ian were rushing enthusiastically about helping to carry the Dawes' things up to the flat. "You might at least take your own things up," Barbara's mother reproached her. "There'll be plenty of time for ponies later."

"Sorry," said Barbara.

"I can carry this box," Ian was saying, heaving one of Barbara's cartons a foot at a time down the hall to the staircase. The carton had not weathered the journey at all well and was bulging ominously and splitting at the seams.

"It's too heavy for you, Ian." Barbara rushed after him, thinking: *my stories.*

"It's quite all right, I'm very strong," said Ian, holding on to the carton by its string and attempting to drag it up the stairs.

"Do be careful, Ian," said his father, coming down-stairs. He, too, grabbed the carton by the string and lifted it casually. There was a loud bang as the string broke and a cascade of books and magazines crashed and slithered downstairs. Barbara watched numbly. Ian began to laugh and cheer loudly.

"Oh dear, Barbara, I'm so sorry, that was entirely my fault," said Mr. Lindsay, leaning against the bannister and laughing.

The crash brought the rest of the two families onto the scene.

"It doesn't matter," said Barbara's mother. She bent to pick up the magazines and noticed one of the brown packages. "The rubbish you carry around with you. What on earth have you got in here?" She drew out one of Barbara's precious manuscripts. "A Horse for Caroline'," she read aloud in an amused voice.

"That's private," Barbara heard herself say loudly.

"You mustn't look at it, it's private." She felt sick and her heart was beating very loudly. She started back down the stairs.

"Don't be silly, I didn't know you'd been writing stories. Horse stories, of course," Barbara's mother flicked through the pages before Barbara reached her and snatched the book from her hand.

"Don't look at it, you mustn't look at it, it's mine." Barbara said in a furious whisper, conscious of everyone watching. "How dare you look at it, you can't bear to leave anything alone! Why can't you mind your own business?" She heard her own voice rising angrily.

"Barbara," said her father. "Go upstairs to your room and don't come down until you can apologize to your mother."

"I think she should apologize to me for looking at my private things without asking," said Barbara trembling.

"Upstairs."

Barbara picked up the other two parcels and some of the books. As she straightened up, her heart still beating hard, she caught sight of Peggy's horrified face, Ian and Tessa's embarrassed ones. She had to take a great gulp of air to stop herself from crying. Her breath came in short bursts and she had to pause once or twice after the first flight of stairs. She had broken out in a sweat and perspiration was running down her back and between her thighs. She had not felt conscious of her fatness all day, but now she saw herself as she must have appeared to the Lindsays, a grotesque, scarlet, gasping lump of lard who couldn't even run upstairs. She reached her room at last, threw down her books and manuscripts, and kicked them in a rage. She sat on the edge of her mattress, gasping for breath, unable to weep, her heart hammering.

"It was clumsy of me to drop that box," said Mr. Lindsay apologetically. His wife shot him a cross but loving look which said, I wish you wouldn't always apologize for everyone. He made a face back at her.

"I'd better go see if she's all right," Mrs. Dawes said quietly.

"Perhaps you'd like to take her a cup of tea," suggested Mrs. Lindsay. "It won't take a minute. Then the children can take the rest of her things up to her."

"That would be kind," said Mrs. Dawes gratefully. "I'm so sorry about this."

Upstairs, she looked with concern at Barbara's flushed face as she handed her a cup of tea. "Are you all right?"

Barbara looked at her mother guardedly. She felt calmer but she was not ready for a confrontation. She sipped the tea. It was very sweet and made her feel better.

"Peggy and Ian are going to bring up your other things in a minute," her mother hesitated. "I don't know why you don't want me to know you write stories. Surely you didn't think I'd be cross."

"They're just private," said Barbara. She took another sip. "They're no good. And I'm not bothered any more. Really. I'll probably throw them out. I wrote them years ago."

"Oh don't throw them away, it'll be fun to read them again when you're older."

Mind your own business, Barbara told her mother silently. She waited for her to go. She wanted to cry. What a rotten beginning. What a baby the Lindsays would think she was.

CHAPTER THREE

Down to Earth

"IT MUST BE marvellous to be able to write," said Peggy a few weeks later as she, Tessa and Barbara steered their ponies at the end of a group that trotted along the forestry path.

"I'm really not very good," said Barbara.

"Write a story about *me*," said Tessa. "I'm going to be the youngest person ever to win an Olympic medal. Younger than Mum. That would make a really good story."

"Jolly boring with you for a heroine," said Peggy.

Barbara was flattered but rather daunted by the way the Lindsays now seemed to take for granted that she was a writer. It had been a great relief to find that the children did not despise her for the scene she had made, but she felt she was a dreadful fraud. She didn't think her efforts were nearly good enough to be regarded as real writing. And, she realized now, she would dearly like to feel that they were.

Perhaps she ought to let Peggy read her stories to see

what she thought of them. That was a drastic step though—what if Peggy laughed? I'll finish "The Blind Pony" and then decide, thought Barbara. Progress had been rather slow recently. Too many other things had been happening.

Looking after Bianca in real life, rather than in her imagination, for one thing. Grooming and feeding her, even dressing her foot, though that was better now. And spending hours in the paddock or the stable just talking to her.

Barbara had never done so much regular riding, either, or enjoyed it so much. (Her father had recently raised her pocket money by a surprisingly generous amount, and neither he nor her mother commented when most of it went to Saturday afternoon rides.) The countryside was wonderful for trekking with plenty of bridle paths leading over stretches of moorland and forest and sudden hidden valleys which surrounded the little town. Barbara would ride dreamily along, gazing at the ever-changing horizon, listening to the gossip of the other riders, the chink of the bits as horses shook their heads, and the unfamiliar calls of the wild birds. It was a totally different world from the short, crowded paths and fierce competitiveness of the urban riding schools she had known.

"Want to canter, Barbara?" Mrs. Lindsay, on Coningsby, was leading the trek that afternoon. She waited with a small group of riders where the forest track opened onto a bare hillside.

Barbara came out of her reverie with a start. "I'm not very good at cantering yet," she said, blushing and clutching nervously at the reins as though her pony might break into a canter there and then.

"Why not have a try? It's an easy canter here; it's uphill so you won't get run away with."

"Oh, go on, cantering is lovely," urged Peggy. "Do have a try."

Tessa was already flapping her arms and legs, pulling her pony about in anticipation. "I'll race you all up there," she said.

"Hold still, Tessa, give the others time to get clear, and stop tormenting your pony."

"Look at that, and she's the one who's going to be the great equestrian," said Peggy.

Suddenly Barbara found herself among the group of riders who wanted to canter. She swallowed nervously and gripped with her thighs and calves as hard as she could.

"Ride alongside me," Mrs. Linday said quietly. "Polka likes Consy, she'll keep pace with him."

Barbara nodded and felt her jaw tighten.

"Sit up a bit," Mrs. Lindsay advised. "Hold the front of your saddle with your left hand if you like. Both reins on your right hand . . ." Mrs. Lindsay reached over. "That's it." She smiled at Barbara. "Okay, Peggy, lead on, no rushing now. *Tessa!*" But Tessa had already urged her pony into a racing gallop, crouched low over its withers. She can certainly stick on, thought Barbara.

"That child!" was all Barbara heard Mrs. Lindsay say before the horses were cantering, and she was lurching about in the saddle, white-faced and terrified. "Sit up!" Mrs. Lindsay called, and Barbara did her best to push herself upright.

For a split second Barbara found her seat and cantered more easily as they reached the brow of the hill. She took a deep breath and began to relax just as Tessa reappeared, out of control, her pony galloping headlong through the others towards Mrs. Lindsay and Barbara. Polka jumped wildly and Barbara flew into the air, hitting the grass with a shattering bump.

"Tessa!" Barbara heard Mrs. Lindsay's furious bellow from far away as she tried to sit up. Her stomach heaved as the impact of the fall echoed through her.

Peggy had jumped off her pony and was running towards her. "Barbara! Are you all right?"

"I think so. B-bit bruised. Trust me to fall off." I'm not going to cry, she told herself. I'm not going to cry.

"Tessa's such a fool, she's upset the whole ride." Peggy crouched down beside Barbara. "Thank goodness nobody else fell off. Mum's *furious.*"

Barbara stood up painfully and swayed a little. Peggy caught hold of her. "Wow, you look pale. That was an awful fall. Are you sure you're all right?"

"Yes," whispered Barbara. Then she said more firmly, "Yes, I'm all right. Shouldn't we catch Polka?" She was not going to admit to Peggy that she had just experienced the most terrifying moment of her life.

The rest of the riders had continued on their way, but Mrs. Lindsay was riding back towards Peggy and Barbara, leading Polka by the reins.

"I am so sorry about that," she said to Barbara. "Are you all right? You look a bit shaky."

"I'm okay," said Barbara, wishing she could go home.

"Want to get on again then? Not too stiff?"

There was nothing to do but to heave herself weakly into the saddle again while Peggy held the off-side stirrup. She wondered if Polka would be jumpy after her fright but she appeared to have reverted to her normal sleepy self. Barbara cautiously sorted out the reins, hoping that Mrs. Lindsay would not notice how her hands trembled.

"That was a pity, you were just beginning to get the hang of cantering," Mrs. Lindsay told her cheerfully. "We'll have to have another go sometime when Madam Tessa isn't about." She rode off to catch up with the other riders while Peggy caught and remounted her own horse.

Peggy said, "Oh Barbara, let's go home, I'm all upset after that, aren't you?"

Barbara nodded thankfully, biting her lip to stop herself from weeping. "I feel like such a fool, falling off like that," she said.

"Crumbs, anyone would have fallen off. You should have seen the way Polka jumped."

But why did it have to happen *just* when I was starting to canter? Barbara asked herself angrily as they rode back to the stable. Something always stops me from cantering. Whatever made me think it would be different here from anywhere else? The memory of the fall and of all the other falls that had preceded it replayed sickeningly across her brain. How she dreaded the next time she went for a ride.

Back at Mount Severn, Peggy said to Barbara, "I'll see to the ponies. Why don't you take Bianca her hay?" She watched Barbara's face anxiously.

"Well, if you don't mind," Barbara tried to catch her breath. "I ought to go and see how she's getting on in the paddock anyway. We don't want her to tread on anything again."

"Seeing as how you practically comb the grass every morning," said Peggy, "I don't think that's likely."

Barbara grinned weakly and started toward the stables. Bianca was standing with her head over the paddock gate as Barbara approached with the fresh hay. Did she see me coming or was she just standing there? wondered Barbara. How much can she really see? She always seems to be waiting for you, to be looking straight at you, yet Miss Brown told us she can't see clearly beyond a few yards. Perhaps she has second sight, Barbara thought, like a phantom horse in one of those Welsh folk tales. There was something about Bianca's soft eyes that made you feel they saw beyond your physical outline, that they looked right into your soul. She sees the real me, thought Barbara, she doesn't notice my being fat.

Bianca stretched her head out for the sugar lump in Barbara's palm. She snorted as she lifted it delicately with her pink lips. Barbara hugged the pony's neck tenderly.

As soon as I saw her, I knew, thought Barbara. I knew instinctively that Bianca would be *the* pony. "One day," she whispered in Bianca's ear, which twitched as if in response, "One day we'll show them, Bianca." She bent to pick up more hay and a twinge of pain shot down her hip and the back of her thigh. At least I got back on again, she told herself, hoisting an armful through the paddock gate and fixing it into place. Carrying hay had become less of an effort lately—could she be getting fitter?—but today it left her feeling rather shaky. She leaned against Bianca's shoulder, her disappointment with herself returning. "What am I going to do? Why am I so hopeless?" she asked Bianca miserably.

Bianca turned from munching wisps of hay to look sympathetically at Barbara.

I'll cut out riding for a bit, thought Barbara, I'll concentrate on my story. I haven't written anything for ages.

Bianca gazed at Barbara and chomped steadily on her mouthful of hay. Her expression seemed to say, we'll never show anyone anything that way, you know.

"We will in the end," she told the pony, unconvincingly.

As the Daweses were eating their tea an hour or so later there was a knock on their living room door and a shame-faced Tessa looked cautiously in. "I've come to say sorry to Barbara," she said. She had changed out of her jodhpurs into a cotton frock which made her look even younger than her eight years.

"What on earth for?" asked Mrs. Dawes. Barbara had not been able to bring herself to tell her mother about her fall, although she was beginning to feel quite stiff and it was hard not to limp.

"It was my fault she fell off this afternoon," explained Tessa. "I'm very sorry Barbara, I hope you didn't hurt yourself, and I won't do it again." She finished in a pleased rush, as though she had been told what to say, and had successfully remembered everything.

"Fell off?" said Barbara's mother. "Are you all right, Barbara?"

"Oh, it was nothing," said Barbara hurriedly. "We were cantering and Tessa's pony frightened Polka, and I fell off. I'm a bit bruised, that's all."

"Ooh, Barbara, can I see? I bet it isn't as big as some of the bruises I've had."

"Little monster!" said Barbara's father, laughing.

Barbara's mother was looking at her carefully. Barbara wondered if she was going to be stern, and say that she thought all this riding was too dangerous.

"Barbara was jolly brave, she got back onto Polka straight away," Tessa told Barbara's mother.

"Oh well, it can't have been too bad then," Mrs. Dawes looked at her daughter, "You're sure you're all right, Barbara."

"Only a bit stiff," said Barbara. "It'll wear off."

"Lord, you horsy people are so stoical," Barbara's father laughed. "One fall would put me off for life."

As if he wasn't always coming home from rugby matches covered with bruises, thought Barbara, surprised and just a little aggrieved that her parents had taken the news of her fall so calmly.

"You aren't cross with me, are you Barbara?" said Tessa.

"Of course not," said Barbara. "But really Tessa you should have been more careful. What about poor old Polka?"

"Susie didn't stop when I told her to," said Tessa, looking shifty.

Watching her Barbara thought, Goodness, she was just as frightened as I was.

"Well, at least you're better at sticking on than me," she said. "Come on, let's go and help Miss Brown with the tack."

"I've got to go anyway, until seven o'clock, for being naughty," said Tessa. "Fancy you wanting to do it for fun."

In the saddle room Miss Brown was sitting at the cluttered table adding up figures in an account book. She looked up as the girls arrived and tutted at Tessa in disapproval.

"What a circus!" she said. "I'm ashamed of you."

"I said I was sorry," said Tessa.

"Humph! I should think so!" Miss Brown's face softened. "Well, you frightened yourself as well, no doubt, so let's hope you've learned your lesson. I don't know. Just like your mother, you are."

"Did Mum get run off with a lot when she was a little

girl?" Tessa climbed onto Miss Brown's knee and gave
her a hug.

"All the time," said Miss Brown. "That Sligo! She
couldn't hold him! And fall off! You never saw anything
like it. Bruises, sprains . . . she even broke her arm
once."

Broke her arm! thought Barbara. And here I am in a
panic because of a bruise.

"She rode him in the end, though. He was really wild,
but she got him jumping," said Tessa dreamily. This was
clearly a familiar story.

"He was a mean old thing," said Miss Brown. "He'd
have been shot if I'd had my way."

"But Mum *trained* him. Look at the prizes they won."

Miss Brown sighed and shook her head. "Prizes aren't
everything, lovey."

Tessa wriggled impatiently on Miss Brown's knee. "I
don't know what you mean," she said crossly.

Intrigued and absorbed, Barbara rubbed slowly at the
saddle she had begun to clean. "Was Sligo Mrs. Lindsay's
first horse?" she asked.

"He was a skewbald," said Miss Brown. "White patches
on a rust coat. Very flashy. And could he jump! But he
came near to killing Nancy. She wouldn't listen to us
though, oh no. She'd have Sligo or no pony at all."

What a *story*, thought Barbara.

"Wait till I get a really good pony," said Tessa.

"No ponies for little girls who gallop about like luna-
tics," said Miss Brown briskly, jumping Tessa off her
knee. "Now then who's supposed to be helping me? Look
at you, leaving it all to Barbara as usual."

"I like it," said Barbara truthfully, busying herself with
saddle soap and cloth once more. The leather was rich

and supple to the touch, and it smelled wonderful, earthy and fresh at the same time.

"You got over your fall all right, Barbara? No broken bones?"

"No-o, just a bit of a bruise."

Miss Brown was watching her gently, almost like Bianca did "No harm in being a bit nervous at first, you know. Better than being overconfident like this naughty girl." Barbara nodded shyly, looking down at her work.

"Best thing would be for you to join in our Saturday morning ladies' class now and again, to go over the basics, like. They're nice ladies. Nearly all beginners and mostly a lot more nervous than you."

She could hardly tell Miss Brown, thought Barbara, that at the moment she felt like putting off the next time she got on a horse for as long as she could. "Thanks awfully. Though," she added, "I'll be busy for a while now. I'm writing a story."

"Don't you put it off for too long now," Miss Brown said firmly. "If at first you don't succeed, try again, isn't it?"

Barbara hardly knew whether Miss Brown was referring to the riding or to the writing. There was no escaping the fact that, either way, she was right. I might as well try, I suppose, Barbara told herself grudgingly. I can't expect everything to come out right at once. And she limped into the house to bed feeling quite brave and pleased with herself.

CHAPTER FOUR

Tessa's Bedtime Story

LATE AFTERNOON on Saturdays people inevitably seemed to gather in the Lindsay living room. Miss Brown, Mrs. Lindsay and the children would come in from feeding the horses after the afternoon ride, Mr. Lindsay and Mr. Dawes would come limping home from playing rugby, and Barbara would be sent to fetch her mother. There was a ritual of watching the sports news on television; Miss Brown's hobby was placing small bets on horse races and she would wait excitedly for the results to be announced, often cheering out loud if she won, then blushing with embarrassment.

This particular Saturday, a few weeks after Barbara's fall, Mr. Lindsay and Mr. Dawes staggered in after a rough game in heavy rain accompanied by "half the forward line," according to Peggy, meaning Phil Williams the policeman ("Goes out with Sybille," Peggy told Barbara), and Gwyn Edwards the school psychologist ("Fancies Sybille"). Despite this, the two men appeared to be friends.

Barbara had heard of Gwyn Edwards. People who reg-

ularly missed school, or bullied the smaller children, or
never spoke to anyone, or were otherwise neurotic, got
sent to him, although she did not know what kind of
treatment he gave them to cure them. He looked quite
friendly—he winked at Barbara. Barbara had never
known a place where people winked at each other so
much.

Mr. Dawes was saying, "Gwyn, this is my wife, Joan."

"Oh yes, the demon librarian," said Gwyn Edwards.
"I've heard all about you, Mrs. Dawes, livening them all
up there. You've got the staff feeling right guilty because
half of them haven't read a book for the last five years."

Barbara's mother laughed, and blushed. Barbara listened in surprise. It had not occurred to her that her
mother might be considered a good librarian. Most of the
children thought she was bossy and very uncooperative
about horse books.

Mrs. Lindsay was having the usual battle with Tessa
about bedtime. Tessa had long been trying to make a
deal: good behavior in return for her own pony. Now
that some time had passed since the runaway pony incident, she had resumed her campaign with exhausting in-
tensity. Everyone wondered how much longer Mrs. Lindsay would be able to hold out before drastically losing her
temper, or giving in. That night, to shorten the agony,
Barbara offered to read Tessa a story and, somewhat to
her surprise, she was accepted. Everyone sighed thankfully as Barbara, feeling virtuous, followed Tessa upstairs. She noticed her mother deep in conversation with
Gwyn Edwards, probably talking about books.

"What about *National Velvet*," said Barbara. "Do you
think it's too old for you?"

"I don't want it," said Tessa. "I want you to read me
one of your books."

"Oh, but you wouldn't like any of them," Barbara said hastily. "They're hopeless really. You'd like *National Velvet* much better."

"No, I wouldn't. I want you to read me your book," said Tessa, bouncing about on her bed, aware that she had Barbara in a corner. "*Your* book, *your* book, I want you to read me *your* book."

"All right, all right," said Barbara, fearing a tantrum. "You asked for it. But you've got to listen properly and not play about."

"I will," said Tessa, still bouncing. "I will, I will."

Down in her room, Barbara rummaged through the chest of drawers. Not the new book, she decided, choosing the earliest one, which was the shortest and had the youngest heroine. Barbara had been eleven when she wrote it, so the heroine was eleven too. It was sixty-three pages long, copied in Barbara's best large handwriting.

"It's too long to read it all at once," Barbara told Tessa. "I'll read you the first chapter and if you think it's okay I'll read you another chapter tomorrow night."

In fact Tessa demanded two chapters that evening, much to Barbara's satisfaction, although it was hard work reading aloud and having to cope with Tessa's constant interruptions. She asked for more information about each new character and horse, and made further suggestions about what could happen to them. Barbara told herself that it was silly to place any value in the opinions of a seven-year-old. Rereading the story she knew that it was hopelessly corny, a jumble of characters and events largely derived from other books she had read, and full of dreadful conversation which had sounded terribly witty when she had first written it. But there was something about it . . . it read like a real story. And Tessa seemed to want to know what happened in the next chap-

ter. Perhaps, thought Barbara, perhaps my stories are
good enough to be regarded as proper writing after all.

Barbara promised to read more to Tessa tomorrow,
tucked her in and took the manuscript thoughtfully back
to her room. She decided that it was time she finished
"The Blind Pony." And perhaps she might even think
about showing it to someone.

A tempting picture of the future formed in her mind,
of Barbara Dawes, the children's novelist who wrote
horse stories which were not immediately categorized as
bad literature.

Barbara hurried downstairs, thinking about these prospects with a little glow of excitement. She wanted to be
alone to think so she went to see Bianca.

Inside the stable it was warm and cozy with the breath
of horses and the insulating depth of their bedding. Two
stalls had been partitioned to make a loose box for
Bianca, next to Coningsby. Bianca was waiting for Barbara, luminous in the light of Barbara's torch, her long
white lashes drooping over her eyes.

Barbara leaned on the partition, stroking Bianca and
thought about the stories she would write. Writing books
seemed a marvellously independent way of life. She
would work at home. She imagined a pretty cottage, with
stables and paddocks. The cottage would have a study
with a mahogany desk by the window overlooking the
garden, and built in glass-fronted bookcases, full of the
books she had written, which would be published in pa-
perback, and in numerous foreign languages.

Her daydreams were interrupted by muffled voices
and the loud bang of the kitchen door. Some people were
coming into the yard. One of them sounded like her
mother. Barbara went quietly to the stable door and took

a quick look. Her mother was still talking to Gwyn Edwards. Their voices carried clearly over to the stable.

"You don't know the lengths she'll go to to get food if she's in that kind of mood," Barbara's mother was saying. 'Stealing food from the larder in the middle of the night, spending all her pocket money on biscuits. She can't seem to stop herself."

Barbara bit furiously at her knuckles, her heart rattling nervously. Gwyn Edwards was the *Psychologist.* Why was her mother telling him all about her? It wasn't neurotic to feel hungry and to enjoy eating. Children in books were always eating enormous meals. Besides, neurotic was only a polite word for mad, and she wasn't mad. Barbara swallowed. Surely her mother didn't think she was mad.

"I wish we had a better relationship. But she seems to resent me," her mother was saying. "It's ironic, isn't it? I'm a children's librarian, I'm supposed to understand kids."

"Well, don't worry too much for now," Gwyn Edwards reassured her. "I know it's no use my saying that, though."

Mrs. Dawes hesitated. "I don't suppose you could have a bit of a chat with her some time? Informally, I mean. She might be more open with you."

"We-ell . . . anything I can do to help, of course." Barbara heard him sigh, as if at a loss. "You know, this child obesity is such a complex thing. Why one kid and not another? Is it a symptom or a cause? I wonder if . . ." his voice was lost in the slam of a car door.

Barbara stood frozen in the stable. How could her mother? She would never forgive her for telling Gwyn Edwards such personal things. She should have realized that home had been a bit too easy to be true recently. And even her new school could not be the easy-going haven it had seemed so far if psychologists waited to pounce on you at every corner. Well, if her mother thought she was going to go to Gwyn Edwards to be probed and examined until her mind did not belong to her anymore, she'd better think again. And the next time he came to Mount Severn and winked at her she'd leave the room.

She climbed into Bianca's box and put her arms round the soft white neck. Bianca was growing a winter coat as fine as angora. She snuffled away and slobbered over Barbara's plaits in a comforting, understanding way, and Barbara began to sob helplessly and angrily into Bianca's mane.

Oh God, why couldn't people leave her alone? She had been so happy. Her weight problem had seemed less menacing and she had even started thinking about dieting herself. People who thought she didn't care about her weight were wrong. She cared desperately; nearly every morning of her life she would say as she got up, I'll try to eat less today. But nearly always by mid-morning she was filled with a panicky hunger. It was this panic that she could not understand. It was far stronger than any vision she might have of herself as slim; in fact the more she felt a miserable failure because she could not get slim, the more she panicked at the prospect of going without food. The thought of all this confusion coming under observation brought out a cold sweat of shame and humiliation. It would be far, far worse than people realizing she was frightened of falling off her horse.

Barbara clutched her head in her hands, overwhelmed. Why was life so unfair?

"Oh, there you are!" Peggy had come into the stable

behind Barbara, flashlight in hand. "Your mother's making supper. She says to tell you it'll be ten minutes." Peggy's voice trailed off as she realized that Barbara was crying.

Barbara turned away and took a deep breath, but she couldn't stifle a last sob. "Okay," she said, fumbling for a handkerchief.

"Oh, I'm sorry," said Peggy awkwardly. "What's wrong?" She shone the light away from Barbara. Tall shadows leapt around the stall and Bianca jerked her head slightly as the beam caught her eyes.

"It's nothing," said Barbara, blinking hard and breathing deeply. Then she burst out suddenly, "It's not fair, she's getting the psychologist onto me now."

"Who is?"

Barbara gave Peggy a look.

"Oh, you mean your Mum." Peggy flicked the light off and on reflectively. "Oh, well, perhaps she thinks you're one of those extra bright types who needs special coaching."

"It's not that. It's because I'm fat. It's a sign of neurosis, didn't you know?" said Barbara angrily. Then, in spite of herself she began to weep again. "Nobody understands, nobody knows what it's like to be nagged and got at every time you put a bite of food into your mouth. It just makes everything worse. And I thought it was so nice here, nobody nagging me."

"Well, we don't," said Peggy. "But I know it must be awful. It's Sybille's big thing, people nagging fat people. She goes absolutely berserk if anyone does at school."

"It isn't the people at school. They've all been okay," said Barbara, sniffing. "You must think I'm an awful baby, crying like this."

"Oh, no, not at all," said Peggy, perfectly sincerely. She had so few problems, she sometimes envied people who had them because she thought it gave them deeper, more interesting characters. Although she felt that Barbara sometimes tried too hard to be nice, and was far too willing to help with even the most dreary tasks, she had long ago decided that Barbara deserved the deep and interesting label rather than the boring and hopeless one.

"Mind you, Gwyn's very nice," said Peggy fairly. "He wouldn't nag you. But why does your Mum want you to see him? Lots of people are a bit fat, it's not a sign that they're mental."

"I don't know," said Barbara, wiping her nose. She didn't want to repeat her mother's complaints about her nighttime raids on the larder. "I think she just wants someone official who'll back her up saying I've got to go on a diet. She wants to get him on her side."

"What I'd do if I were you," said Peggy, "is go and have a chat with Sybille about it. She's friends with Gwyn Edwards, I told you he fancies her. I bet she'd be willing to ask him not to bother you with dieting and things."

Barbara considered this and began to feel better. She smiled damply at Peggy.

"You don't think she'd mind?" she asked.

"Gosh, no, of course not. She always says it's her campaign to stop fat people being victimized. Besides, she loves to show off her cottage to anyone that turns up." Peggy started towards the door. "It's worth going to see, actually. Why don't you walk down tomorrow afternoon? Sunday is usually a good time to find her in."

"Oh," said Barbara nervously, feeling rushed. "Well, perhaps I will. Oh, blow it, I will." She smiled gratefully at Peggy. They stood at the stable door and looked at the starry sky, suddenly shy with one another.

"You'd better go in, your Mum will be wondering where you are."

"Are my eyes very red?"

Peggy shone the flashlight. "Can't really tell. You can have a wash in our bathroom if you like."

"Thanks.—Peggy, you won't tell anyone, will you? If my mother knew I'd heard her talking to Gwyn Edwards—"

"Of course not. What do you think I am?"

"Well I knew you wouldn't really." said Barbara. She stuffed her handkerchief back in her pocket. "Look, I'll just give Bianca some nuts. I wasn't very good company for her tonight." Rashly she added, "I'm writing a story about Bianca. I've nearly finished it. It's not very good but you can read it if you like."

"Gosh, did you? Can I really? But I thought you didn't like people reading your stories."

Barbara felt off balance. She hadn't meant to say so much. "Well, I don't usually. But Tessa made me read one of my first ones at bedtime tonight. I thought you could be a critic and tell me if it's any good or not."

Barbara began to tell Peggy about "The Blind Pony" as they went indoors. She was filled with the sense of having burned her bridges, of being committed. She thought about it throughout supper, and afterwards as she washed up and ate leftovers in the kitchen. She began to see being a writer as the only possible career in which she could be independent and answerable to no one about what she did or ate. But, she thought, surely somewhere on the way towards this freedom her weight problem would solve itself. She could not really believe that she might still be fat when she was thirty.

CHAPTER FIVE

Sidesaddle

BARBARA couldn't think of an excuse to avoid the adult beginners' riding class the next morning. All week she had been dreading getting on a horse again, but this fear had been completely swamped by the drama of the previous evening. She woke up early, ate a solitary, hearty breakfast, and rushed outside eagerly to help Miss Brown in the stables, thankful to forget her bitter feelings about her mother for a while. She carried bales of hay and buckets of water, helped catch the horses that were still left out at night, and brushed the worst of the mud from their thickening coats.

Bianca was turned out in the nearest paddock for the day but leaned over the gate to nod her head and whinny at any pony or person who went near her. She's so vulnerable, Barbara thought. She's so sweet-natured and trustful yet the world must seem strange and misty to her. It was fortunate that she was here at Mount Severn where everyone loved her and would not dream of hurting her. It was not so easy being a person. You had to learn to protect your vulnerable areas on your own.

Gwydion, the dark brown Welsh cob, was standing in the yard, tied up by his headcollar. He was a deep-bodied, compact horse of fourteen hands, as substantial as a small carthorse in his winter coat.

"Gosh! Who's riding sidesaddle?" asked Barbara, as Miss Brown came out of the tack-room, very pink-faced from carrying the strange equipment. Barbara rushed to help.

Miss Brown giggled, showing her large teeth. "Why, that old Sybille, I don't know what she'll think of next." She gratefully relinquished half of the saddle to Barbara and tried to imitate Sybille's melodious voice. " 'I'll show the Lindsays the way to make a fat bottom look good on the back of a horse,' she said. 'What was good enough for Queen Victoria is good enough for me.' " Barbara couldn't help laughing, too. " 'Get that sidesaddle out, Miss Brown,' she says to me," Miss Brown continued, " 'let's give the Mount Severn stables a bit of style.' "

"Gosh! But has she ever ridden sidesaddle? Is it hard to learn?"

"It makes your back ache at first, if you learn properly. You sit on your right hip, like. But it's easy to stay on with your leg hooked round the pommel." Miss Brown mimed illustratively, and giggled again. "I told her she'd need to wear some tough old breeches but she said, not on your life, she was going to make a new outfit special. I don't know what it'll be like I'm sure."

Together Barbara and Miss Brown heaved the cumber-some saddle onto Gwydion's back and Miss Brown darted about fastening the girth and the balance strap. Finally giving the single nearside stirrup a tug, she smiled, "There, she should be able to get up all right."

"Poor old Gwydion looks disgusted," said Barbara.

Miss Brown took Gwydion's bridle and looked him sternly in the eye. "It'll give him something to think about for a change. He's an old soldier, he is."

Apart from Barbara there were six other people in the class today, women friends who worked in town. They began to arrive just before ten, dressed in very smart trousers and sweaters. They chatted cheerfully as they tried on the hard hats required for riding lessons, from the faded pile of spares in the tack-room.

Barbara had already mounted the lazy brown mare, Polka, so that the other riders would not observe her inept heave into the saddle. Polka had a sharp backbone so at least the saddle did not slip round too far as Barbara hauled herself up. Even so it always took several attempts before she managed to spring high enough to get her right leg over.

Once in the saddle Barbara felt more secure. She turned Polka so that she could inspect herself in the kitchen window. She felt neat and not too bulky in her fawn corduroy trousers and matching smock over her blue sweater. Her crash cap was brown and fitted neatly over her braids. She felt right. She practiced gripping the saddle with her thighs and calves; it seemed easy enough when the horse was standing still. Let it be all right today, she prayed. Don't let me fall off.

Just as the other six women were settling down into their saddles and were having their position corrected by Miss Brown, a car tore up Fron Lane and turned into the yard, scattering the gravel. The trekking ponies were all traffic proof and did no more than flick their ears. Phil Williams, the policeman, got out of the driver's seat and Sybille stepped from the passenger's side in a swirl of long skirts.

"Why didn't you open the door for me, varlet," she said
to Phil. She straightened up slowly.

Everyone in the yard stared at her, and she smiled
smugly at her audience.

She looked spectacular. Her dark hair was piled up under a grey bowler hat. She wore a tight, grey jacket with
scarlet piping which emphasized the curves of her plen-
tiful figure. A matching skirt, full and sweeping, fell to
her ankles and revealed black, side-buttoned leather
boots. A white stock about her neck and grey kid gloves
completed the outfit.

The noise of her arrival had brought all the other oc-
cupants of Mount Severn into the yard.

"Sybille!" screamed Peggy. "Fantastic!"

"I don't know where you think you're going, dressed
like that, Hyde Park or something," scolded Miss Brown.
"I told you trousers would do to start with."

"Oh, don't, Miss Brown," Sybille swished up the path.
"I wanted to see how it looked. Phil can take my photo.
Not bad for home-made, don't you think?" She held up
her full skirts and twirled about. "Mind you, I'm corseted
to death. I shall probably expire within half an hour. But
do you realize this is the first waist I've ever had?"

The Lindsays and Barbara's father were saying,
"Wow," and whistling and laughing. Mrs. Dawes stood in
the kitchen doorway looking stunned. Barbara sat on
Polka's back and stared, lost in admiration. Sybille looked
fabulous, there was no other word for it. How she dared!
And she had made the outfit herself. All the ordinary
slim women in the yard, even Mrs. Lindsay, were well
and truly upstaged.

"Now then, Sybille, let's see you get on," said Mrs.
Lindsay, leading Gwydion to the mouting block. "Don't

just stand there, Phil, come and do your knight in shining armor act. Why didn't you make him a costume while you were at it, Sybille?"

"Well, I did suggest a kilt, but he was afraid someone from the rugby team might see him."

"Do you want me to carry on with the others while you show Sybille what to do, Miss Brown?" asked Mrs. Lindsay. "You're the sidesaddle expert."

"Thank you, Nancy," said Miss Brown, looking relieved. She must have been worried that her other customers might be getting restless. But they were gazing at Sybille and laughing like everyone else. Good old Sybille, thought Barbara, she's really waving the flag for fat people.

"Hey, I don't want to spend all morning riding around on my own," said Sybille. "I'll follow the class in a minute. How do I mount this animal, Miss Brown?" Lifting her skirts, she climbed to the top step of the mounting block and stood waiting.

"Come along," said Mrs. Lindsay to the rest of the class. "We'll go to the bottom paddock where we won't be distracted." She started herding the class out. "I'm sorry the lesson is late starting but we'll see that you get your full hour."

"Spoilsport," Sybille called after her. Mrs. Lindsay grinned back and made a face.

Barbara managed to hang back long enough to see Sybille mount. She did not seem to have any trouble. It was the arrangement of her skirt which took the time. She's taller than me, thought Barbara, so she doesn't look so fat. She can get away with it. Perhaps I will too if I grow taller.

The class was almost over when Sybille and Gwydion

trotted jerkily across the flat roadside paddocks to join them, followed by Miss Brown. The riders had been walking and trotting in sedate circles and over poles on the ground, occasionally taking their feet out of the stirrups. This had not proven to be as nerve-racking as Barbara had feared; by the end of the lesson she felt confident enough to do it without holding on to the pommel of the saddle. She still slithered around when they trotted, though. But, she thought hopefully, her balance seemed to be improving, even if her grip was not. She thought she had light hands; she did not hang on by the reins.

The class watched Sybille's arrival with interest. "It's wonderful," she told them. "You're absolutely wedged on, you can't possibly fall off."

"You got to learn to keep your back straight," said Miss Brown breathlessly. "You mustn't let yourself slip round to the nearside, Sybille, or you'll drag the saddle over."

"Yes, but when I do that my left buttock has nothing to sit on."

The class tittered, and Sybille grinned at them. Mrs. Lindsay watched with a sardonic smile. "That's how it should be. It takes some getting used to."

Barbara watched Sybille carefully as she joined the class. She looked very grand, sitting (enthroned, Barbara thought, was the best way to describe it) on the high saddle, her skirts flowing along Gwydion's near side. She also looked very safe; she rode on a long rein but it seemed right for her. Barbara wondered if she dare ask Miss Brown if she could try sidesaddle one day. It would be marvellous to be able to canter and gallop without any fear of falling off.

As they rode back to the yard after the class, other

women let their horses jostle around Sybille and Gwydion. They all asked her eagerly how it felt to ride sidesaddle.

"Don't start a fashion, Sybille," laughed Mrs. Lindsay. "We can't afford to buy any more sidesaddles."

"Oh Nancy," said one of the women, "And I was just going to ask if anyone could have sidesaddle lessons."

"It looks so lovely," said another, "I've always fancied myself in a green velvet riding habit like Scarlet O'Hara."

"Or Queen Elizabeth the First on a white palfrey," said someone else. "And you've got a white pony, haven't you, Nancy? You'll have to get it a sidesaddle."

"Give the poor thing a chance, she's only two," Mrs. Lindsay smiled.

Barbara was annoyed to hear Bianca being discussed by these people, especially to hear her being described as a white palfrey—this was her own idea. But she was stirred by the romantic picture of herself in a green velvet costume riding a full-grown Bianca in a velvet-covered sidesaddle. Green suited Barbara's coloring and her auburn hair; all her best clothes, such as they were, were green. Not that she could imagine the occasion for which such an outfit would be suitable, except a pageant or a fancy dress competition. Barbara could not see herself as another Sybille, dressing up extravagantly for the sheer fun of it.

She had begun to lose her nerve about visiting Sybille. She was afraid Sybille would mock her and tell her to take a more positive attitude. She felt, too, that her new ambition to be a writer ought to be good enough armor against nagging parents and interfering educational psychologists. Barbara had been relieved, therefore, when Sybille arrived with Phil Williams. It seemed to mean that they were spending the day together, and she would have to postpone her visit to the cottage. However, back in the yard, there was no sign of Phil or his car. Then Barbara overheard Sybille telling Peggy's mother that he had gone on duty, and he'd probably be in trouble for being late.

"Well, stay to lunch if you aren't doing anything," suggested Mrs. Lindsay. She dismounted neatly and led her horse over to where Sybille sat atop Gwydion.

"Thanks a lot, but I really ought to get home. The place looks like the town dump at the moment." Sybille sniffed dramatically. "Besides," she said, tugging at her waist, "I need to get out of this damn corset before I pass out altogether. And that woman asks me if I'm eating! One thing, it helps to support your back. Put me down for next Sunday as well," she called to Miss Brown. "I can see I'm going to get quite hooked on horse riding, just like Barbara." She winked across the paddock at Barbara, who blushed. "You ought to try the sidesaddle, Barbara."

"Barbara's doing fine as she is," Mrs. Lindsay said. "Now let's see if you can dismount like a lady, you strumpet." Sybille kicked her left foot out of the stirrup, unhooked her right leg and sprang neatly to the ground. For a large person she was unexpectedly light on her feet. "That do, teacher?" She stretched and wriggled. "Wow, am I going to be stiff tomorrow." Sybille walked around a bit. "Don't look at me in that tone of voice, Gwydion, I've got a lump of sugar for you in my skirt pocket. Pockets too," she added, showing them off.

"Where did you get that pattern, Sybille?" asked one of the women. "It's beautiful material, too." There was a murmur of agreement and Sybille became involved in a discussion about cutting and fitting and how to make piped seams neatly, which Peggy hastened to join. Barbara went with Miss Brown and Mrs. Lindsay to unsaddle and rub down the horses. Miss Brown and Mrs. Lindsay were laughing and making faces over Sybille's performance.

"But still, it's something to think about," Mrs. Lindsay was saying, as she groomed quickly under Coningsby's tummy. "It might be quite a draw in the summer to offer sidesaddle lessons. Shades of the gracious past and all that. If we could find more saddles—don't they have to make them to measure to fit you and the horse, or something?"

"I think it would be lovely," said Barbara, hovering with an armful of saddlery. "I'd love to ride sidesaddle. It's so romantic and historic. I think Sybille looked marvellous."

"That's not a proper habit," said Miss Brown. "She should wear breeches and an apron to be correct."

"Not nearly as glamorous, though," said Mrs. Lindsay, straightening up. She gave Coningsby a friendly slap on the quarters and moved on to do Polka. "And heaven knows what a proper habit would cost nowadays," she continued. "That full skirt will suit the purpose for Sybille. She's only going in for it to have a laugh and cause a stir." She bent to pick up Polka's feet.

Barbara hastened to the tackroom with her burden. "Do people still ride sidesaddle? Seriously, I mean," she asked.

"Well, I have heard that it's coming back into fashion among the rich," said Mrs. Lindsay with a teasing smile.

"It's quite good for people who are a bit nervous," said Miss Brown kindly, handing Barbara another saddle. "It's much harder to fall off even at the gallop."

"And of course, it looks much more elegant, especially for those of the, er, Juno-esque build," said Mrs. Lindsay.

Barbara said defensively, "Sybille looked super. It must

be marvellous for big people to be able to ride without someone saying how they bounce about and how awful they look in tight jodhpurs."

"True, I suppose." Peggy's mother smiled at Barbara suddenly. "But look, love, don't go building Sybille up into a big heroine. She'll lead you astray."

"I'm not," said Barbara, blushing indignantly. That's just the kind of thing grownups tell you about people who do their own thing and don't give a damn, she thought. Really, she was quite disappointed in Mrs. Lindsay.

"Don't get me wrong," said Mrs. Lindsay quickly, seeing Barbara's expression. "Sybille's great. I admire her. But her style's her own, you know."

"Mmm," said Barbara, not altogether mollified. She dumped the last saddle in the tackroom and returned with grooming tools. She set to work with the body brush on the chestnut pony, Susie. Barbara started puffing rather hard as she concentrated on the sweat mark where the saddle had been.

"How did the lesson go?" asked Miss Brown from the other end of the stable. "Enjoy it?"

"Oh yes, thank you," said Barbara, grooming Susie's back. "I'm still not very good at trotting, though."

"Stop running yourself down, girl," said Mrs. Lindsay. "You're doing okay."

She's just saying that, thought Barbara. But she could not help feeling pleased. Perhaps I am improving a bit, she thought.

Barbara and her mother had a row at lunchtime.

"I couldn't believe it," Mrs. Dawes began, spooning out the potatoes. "All that noise this morning. I thought there'd been an accident."

Barbara passed her father the milk and said nothing.

"I drop what I'm doing and rush downstairs all bothered and worried," Barbara's mother gestured with her fork, "and what is it? It's that Sybille!" Mrs. Dawes snorted. "I read somewhere that people act like that because they feel bad about themselves, inferior . . ."

Barbara banged her glass of orange juice angrily on the table. Some of it slopped onto the tablecloth.

"Barbara," her mother sounded annoyed.

"Well it's your fault," cried Barbara furiously. "You can't stand to see anyone enjoying themselves, anyone doing anything out of the ordinary—" Barbara caught her father's exasperated eye but continued anyway, "especially if they look different." She glared defiantly at her mother.

"Fat, you mean," snapped her mother. "Let me tell you there's a good deal of difference between looking unconventional and looking fat and sloppy."

"Leave it, leave it," groaned Barbara's father. "If we're going to start this bickering at mealtimes again, I shall ask the Lindsays if I can eat with them. Besides, it's not fair to say that Sybille looked sloppy, Joan. She looked pretty good, I thought."

"That's why she's mad," Barbara sniffed. "Fat people aren't allowed to look good, it's against the law."

"And *you* can shut up too and not be so rude to your mother."

The meal finished in a hostile silence. Afterwards, Barbara's father rose and said he would be back by five at the latest.

"I don't know why you have to do this wretched training *every* Sunday afternoon," Mrs. Dawes complained. "It would be nice if we could all go together somewhere as a family for a change."

"Well, we can do that if you like, one weekend. But you'd like to see me on the team, wouldn't you?"

Mrs. Dawes said, "Rugby," in a tone Barbara would have sympathized with if she had not been feeling so antagonistic towards her mother. She's just an old dog in the manger, Barbara thought.

CHAPTER SIX

Advice from Sybille

SYBILLE'S COTTAGE was about a mile out of the town, set back from the road and approached by a stony path. It stood at the edge of a wood and was surrounded by a large, t͟a garden which Sybille had already begun to cut back a͟n͟d replant. The cottage was a grey-stoned, one-story building with a slate roof. The small window frames sparkled with new white paint and the front door was a rich dark blue with a brass knocker.

Barbara lurked about on the road near the gate. She felt nervous and silly. She was trying to figure out what she would say to Sybille when suddenly the front door opened and Sybille herself looked out. She had changed out of her riding habit into a long red wool caftan. When she saw Barbara, she waved.

"Hello! Come in and have a look at my palatial abode."

One of the things you could not help liking about Sybille was that out of school she never treated you like a child, however bad a pupil you were. But it was no use thinking that because of this you could take liberties in school. Sybille in school was a different creature, distant and terrifying.

"Hello," said Barbara, relieved that Sybille thought she had merely passed the cottage while out for a walk. "Yes, I'd like that," she said, opening the gate. "Peggy was saying how lovely your cottage is. She said she helped decorate it."

"Yes she did, she's got some good ideas. She'll make a good interior decorator." Sybille stepped back from the door, smiling. "Come on in, I've just been tidying up."

The front door opened onto a low-ceilinged living room with whitewashed beams and a large fireplace in which a log fire burned. The white painted stone walls were hung with richly colored woven rugs and macrame' hangings, and there were more rugs and cushions on the floor and thrown over the chairs and the divan. Shelves in the corner of the room by the fireplace held a large collection of books, mainly paperbacks.

"It's lovely," said Barbara inadequately. It's as warm and comfortable as a rabbit warren, she thought.

"My little nest!" said Sybille. She lifted the old-fashioned latch on one wooden door and Barbara looked through to a cottage-y bedroom—complete with pink roses on the curtains and a white crocheted cover on the bed. A door at the opposite end of the living room led into the kitchen where there were more white beams, a large black kitchen range and a Welsh dresser laden with blue china. It was all so much what Barbara had pictured for herself that she almost felt cheated. She did not want her house to be an imitation of anyone's, not even Sybille's.

"Sit down and I'll make some coffee," said Sybille as Barbara exclaimed over the cottage. She went into the kitchen and returned a few minutes later with a tray laden with flowered china mugs, a kettle, a jar of coffee, milk in a bottle and a plate with a fruit cake on it. "I baked this cake in the oven of the range; I hope it's come out all right." She set the tray down on the rug in front of the fire. "I was going to have the range torn out," Sybille said, dropping onto a floor cushion by the hearth and tucking her feet under her. "But it seemed a shame, seeing as it's part of the original cottage. I'm glad I kept it now."

Barbara sank back into her cushion-filled chair and watched Sybille pour boiling water into the coffee mugs. "It must be a marvellous feeling to have a place that's really your own," she said. "It's what I want more than anything." Barbara paused, gathering her courage, and blurted, "I can't wait to leave school and be independent, and have a house of my own and write books and breed ponies. Then no one will be able to go on at me because I'm too fat and I ought to diet."

Sybille listened to this with raised eyebrows and a broad smile. "Nobody's going on at you here, love," she said. "Have a piece of cake." She took a slice herself and bit into it. "Hm, not bad."

Barbara looked down at her mug of coffee. She noticed with some surprise that her heart was pounding. "I'm sorry," she said, reddening. "To come out with all that, I mean."

"Don't worry," said Sybille, sipping her coffee. "I know how these things build up inside you. I used to get into exactly the same state when I was your age. My grandmother was the worst." She leaned forward and put her cup on the floor. "She used to watch everything I ate, oozing self-righteous disapproval." Sybille laughed and tossed back her hair. "She'd always leave little bits of food on the side of her plate just to show me." Sybille took another large bite of cake. "Well, Nain, this one's for you."

"Nain?" Barbara was puzzled. She took another bite herself.

"That's what Welsh people call their grannies. Haven't you heard Peggy?"

Sybille jumped to her feet and stepped over the floor cushions to the bookshelves. She took down a large, black-bound volume which had been doing duty as a bookend. Sitting on the arm of Barbara's chair, Sybille opened the album, quickly catching at several loose photographs that slipped out. "There she is, the old dragon. And there's me, look. I was, what—sixteen?—when that was taken. A lot bigger than I am even now. You're a beanpole by comparison."

Barbara looked carefully at the smudgy photograph of a huge girl with masses of hair and a ferocious expression. I'm not nearly as fat as that, she thought, impressed.

"What a sight I look in that gym suit," said Sybille. "Mind you I was going through a really aggressive phase at the time. I was so furious because despite being ten times as bright as anyone else at school—well, pretty bright anyway—I was labelled a problem because I was fat."

"It was awful at my last school." Barbara looked up at Sybille. "They tried to get us to join a club. The fat ones, I mean. It's not so bad here, thank goodness. I thought even my mother had stopped bothering about it, but . . ." Barbara hesitated. Despite her anger at her mother she did not want to sound disloyal.

"Your Mum's trying to diet you, is she," Sybille said, leafing slowly through the album.

"She's always doing that," said Barbara. "It's not only that." The memory of last night's conversation came flooding back and she rushed on. "I heard her talking to Gwyn Edwards. They were in the yard and I was in the stable with Bianca; they didn't know I was there. They were talking about me, and my mother wants him to see me because I'm no good at dieting." Barbara felt her eyes well up. "It's not fair, it's not fair that your character should be judged on whether you're fat or not. I'm not doing badly at school and I don't play truant or anything . . ." she trailed off hopelessly.

"Cheer up and have some more coffee," Sybille said. "I'll fill up the kettle." Sybille swung lightly out of the room and Barbara took a deep breath and blinked hard.

"You've got the wrong end of the stick about psychologists," Sybille called from the kitchen. "They don't just lock up mental cases, you know. They're as much shoulders to cry on as anything." She came back and replaced the kettle on the fire. "Gwyn probably told your Mum not to worry. And you needn't worry that he'll be trying to waylay you unless you start doing really strange things. He's got more tact than that. He's quite an understanding guy really."

Barbara listened uncertainly. Had she over-reacted? "It won't make any difference even if he did tell her not to worry," she said, sulking a little. "She definitely thinks I'm a problem because I'm fat."

"We're all pretty brainwashed by this fat business," said Sybille, looking calmly across at her. "Especially our generation—mine and your Mum's. Thin equals good, fat equals bad. It's not surprising we're all neurotic about it."

"You aren't."

"We-ell," Sybille pulled a wry face. "I have my moments." She reached for another piece of cake and continued, "But no, when I left college I made up my mind that I was going to stop persecuting myself for not getting thin like everyone else and just be myself." She took a healthy bite of the cake. "People who didn't like me could lump me," she munched her cake and grinned at Barbara.

Suddenly she reached over for the photograph album again, and turned the pages until she came to several pictures of a thin dark man in swimming trunks. Barbara leaned forward to get a better look over Sybille's shoulder. The man looked rather old to Barbara and not particularly handsome but he had marvellous laughing eyes.

"He gave me faith in myself," said Sybille. "My one and only Frenchman. Gerard." She rolled her tongue voluptuously round the name. "Heavenly man. I met him when I did my year in France, for my degree." She giggled. "Much as it kills me to admit that a *man* could make any difference. Ah, those were the days! I wonder what he's doing now, the blackguard."

Barbara listened, scandalized and envious at the same time. "It would be incredible to think that being fat *really* doesn't matter," she said.

"It's not healthy to be really huge, of course," said Sybille, closing the album on her lap. "That's what worries your Mum, I daresay."

"I suppose so," said Barbara grudgingly.

Sybille stared reflectively into the fire. "But what price your mental state . . ." She turned and smiled up at Barbara. "Don't think I haven't gone through all this hundreds of times. Of course it's nice to be thin and fit. But if dieting makes you miserable it's a waste of time in my opinion. All it does is keep you at home brooding while your life's passing by outside."

"That's what I tell myself," said Barbara eagerly. "But I can't help thinking all the time that perhaps I ought to diet, and then I get into a sweat over should I, shouldn't I, and then I can never keep it up anyway and I get into a sweat about *that*. And then when people are watching you all the time—"

"I know, I know, I was just the same," said Sybille, laughing. "But there's no easy solution you know. It's hard to have faith in yourself but that's what you've got to do. Accentuate the positive, and all that. At least you're in a strong position there." She rose to put the album back.

"What do you mean?"

"You've got an aim in life—an ambition. That's more than most people have, I can tell you." She stood at the bookshelves and looked at Barbara. "Don't you want to be a writer?"

"Oh, yes!"

"There you are, then. Go after it! That's your priority."

Barbara nodded excitedly, her mood soaring. Yes, that's right, she thought, writing is my priority. She began to feel confident and optimistic, determined to look to the future and not to worry about anyone, even her mother. "You don't know what a relief it is to talk to you," she told Sybille. "You've really helped me to sort things out."

"It's a pleasure. Any time. Get your moral support here," said Sybille cheerfully crossing to Barbara's chair.

"Don't worry, girl, when you're writing best sellers it won't matter if you weigh two hundred pounds. Look at Gertrude Stein."

Barbara hurried home in the cold early evening, speculating elatedly about the glamorous future. She wondered who Gertrude Stein was and decided to look in the library for one of her books. Barbara wondered if her mother had heard of her.

After settling Bianca for the night with more bedding and hay and water, she hurried upstairs to the flat. Tea was being prepared, and her father was teasing her mother about the rugby team, telling her that she ought to come and watch the matches. Barbara's mother shuddered. "Where on earth have you been?" she said to Barbara, noticing her flushed face.

"I went for a walk and Sybille showed me round her cottage." Barbara took off her jacket and went to help set the table. "It's fantastic! You ought to go down."

"Yes, I keep meaning to," said Mrs. Dawes, who had spent most of the afternoon regretting her remarks at lunchtime. "We might look for an old place to do up ourselves."

"Ooh, yes, somewhere with a paddock," said Barbara.

"That's an idea, I could bring the team round for training," said her father, winking at Barbara as her mother groaned.

After tea Barbara went upstairs to read to Tessa. Her mood was reinforced by Tessa's enthusiastic reactions. She questioned Barbara relentlessly and demanded two extra chapters.

"I'll read you the new one I've written, if you like," said Barbara, closing her notebook. "It's got a pony in it rather like Bianca. I got the idea that first day we came to see you in the summer."

"Oh goody," said Tessa. "What happens to her?"

"Wait and see," said Barbara, turning off the light. She smiled to herself and hastened to her room to start on the next chapter.

CHAPTER SEVEN

First Book to the Publisher

IN FACT Barbara read aloud the story of the blind pony to all three Lindsay children, piled cosily on Tessa's high, old-fashioned iron bed, every evening for the following week. The story was not very long and by Saturday night she had reached the last chapter in which the heroine and the nearly-cured blind pony win the Pony Club's One-Day-Event. She had gotten quite carried away when she wrote about the competition—she had only finished it that afternoon—and she noticed with surprise and satisfaction that her audience listened with bated breath to this part. They all sighed with pleasure when the last page was reached and the red rosette was fastened to the blind pony's bridle.

"That was really good," said Peggy. She sat up against the wall and hugged her knees to her chest. "You're so clever, Barbara, I don't know how you think of what to write. I bet you'll really be famous when you grow up."

"It's not very good, really," replied Barbara modestly. She straightened the loose pages of her now very bat-

tered notebook and thought about the furious writing
that had gone into finishing the story over the past few
days. "I'm glad you enjoyed it," she said. "I'll make my
neat copy now. I wish I could type so I could make it look
really professional."

"I liked the part where Susan said she didn't want any
pony except Snowmist," said Tessa. Susan and Snowmist
were the names Barbara had given to her heroine and
the blind pony. "You could see she really believed that
Snowmist would beat all the others in the end."

"Oh, no, she didn't do it because of that, she did it because she loved Snowmist more than any of the other
ponies," said Barbara.

"It would be marvellous if it could happen in real life,"
said Peggy, wriggling into a more comfortable position
on Tessa's bed. "Bianca might get better eyesight as she
grows older, Miss Brown says. And there's nothing else
wrong with her, so there's no reason why people
shouldn't be able to ride her."

"That's what Barbara hopes," said Ian. He was very
shrewd. "Susan's a bit like you, isn't she, Barbara? It's a
bit of a dream-come-true story, isn't it?" The bedsprings
twanged as he climbed to the floor. "Things like that
don't happen in real life."

"It's only meant to be a story," said Barbara stiffly. "But
sometimes things like that *do* happen. Look at your
mother. If anyone in a book ends up winning an Olympic
medal everyone says how unrealistic, but your mother did
win a medal, didn't she?"

"Yes, but it didn't happen by magic. And you'd need
magic to make Bianca see properly." Ian hitched himself
onto the edge of the bed again. "And even if we did give
her to you like the people give Snowmist to Susan in the

book, you'd never be able to ride her because you're too fat."

"*Ian!*" Peggy climbed over Tessa's legs toward him. "Just because Barbara's written a story and she got her ideas from real people doesn't mean that she expects what happens in the book to happen to her. And," she prodded her brother, "say sorry to Barbara for making personal remarks."

"Sorry, Barbara," said Ian equably. "But it's a good sign that I feel like that, isn't it? It means that the story's realistic."

Barbara was disturbed by the way Ian seemed to see through her. She sat brooding. She told herself that she had grown out of the fantasy about being given Bianca and riding her to success. She had come to terms with her fatness, she said to herself, and had decided to concentrate upon being a writer instead of an expert horsewoman. But she was surprised to feel a sense of loss and disappointment. For the first time in what seemed ages the old picture of herself, slim and agile on a fast, lively horse sprang into her mind. She tried to replace it with a picture of herself sitting at a mahogany desk writing horse stories, with the brood mares grazing in the paddocks outside, but this was only a different picture, not a substitute one. It's not fair, she thought irritably, why is everything so confusing.

"You are horrible, Ian," Peggy was whispering crossly. "You've hurt Barbara's feelings."

Barbara pulled herself out of her thoughts. "I'm not offended," she said to Peggy. "Really, I was only thinking over what you said about the story," she lied. "Perhaps I ought not to give it such a happy ending. Perhaps I'll write another chapter in which Susan and Snowmist are riding home in triumph and they get killed by a drunken driver. Not even my mother could say it was wish-fulfillment then," she added crossly.

There was a horrified silence. "I didn't mean it," Barbara said hurriedly. "I only wanted you to see that it's only an ordinary story, not something I want to happen to myself."

"But it would be realistic then," said Ian, sliding off the edge of the bed again. "Bianca's quite likely to get run over if she ever gets out onto the road. She wouldn't know what all those fast things coming at her were. Perhaps the pony could be killed and not the girl."

"Oh you," said Peggy. She seized Tessa's pillow and hit him with it. "How awful, how could you, Ian? Oh, don't change the end, Barbara, you can't, I couldn't bear it."

"I think that's what I'll do," said Tessa, coming out of an uncharacteristic reverie. "I'll get Mum to let me break Bianca in and I bet I'll be able to teach her to jump. She'll be at least fifteen hands when she's grown up, Mum says. Perhaps she'll turn out to be a marvellous jumper. I wouldn't need to buy a pony of my own then."

Tessa was beginning to give up hope of being given her own pony in the near future. Her latest scheme was to save up to buy one of the cheap rough ponies which were frequently sold in the local market. By saving up her pocket money and doing odd jobs she had calculated that she would have twenty pounds in a year's time. "If I had Bianca, I could use the twenty pounds for a new saddle," she said now.

"Oh, don't be silly, Tessa, she'll never be able to see properly," said Barbara, jealous and annoyed at the possibility of Tessa usurping her own relationship with Bianca. "Who's getting the story mixed up with real life now?"

"If you copied the story out really neatly and sent it to a publisher," said Peggy, ignoring Tessa, "they might publish it and then you'd be famous. You'd get lots of money too." Peggy retrieved Tessa's pillow and plumped it. "Wouldn't it be super? You could buy a really fantastic pony. Oh you must try, Barbara, your book's just as good as lots of others I've read."

Barbara had already thought of doing this but felt that to say so would make her sound conceited. "It's not really good enough," she said, climbing off the bed and straightening her stiff knees. "But it might be a good idea to try because the publishers would be able to tell me if it's worth writing any more."

Making a neat copy of the book took up much of Barbara's time for the rest of that term. During the Christmas holidays it gave her a convenient excuse for spending much of her time in her room out of her mother's way. And when her mother asked her what she was doing all the time up there, Barbara replied, "Making the final draft of my book."

"It would be nice to see it some time," said her mother casually.

"You wouldn't like it," said Barbara, "It's just for children really." But she felt mean saying it. Some time had passed since the conversation between her mother and Gwyn Edwards, yet her mother hadn't started nagging again about dieting. Her mother was not even making her usual sarcastic remarks about what Barbara ate, and if Gwyn Edwards had been looking for her she had certainly not seen him. Perhaps Sybille had been right about him being too tactful to seek Barbara out deliberately. Still, Barbara thought she must not let herself be lulled into a false sense of security.

Meanwhile, Barbara was still helping in the stables, still taking special responsibility for Bianca and still being gently but firmly pressured by Miss Brown to join the adult beginners' class on Saturday mornings. "I really can't afford it every week," she had told Miss Brown after the second lesson.

"Not to worry about that," Miss Brown had replied. "You've earned your lessons with all the work you do. A big help to me you are."

Free riding lessons in return for help in the stables would have seemed like a dream come true to Barbara back in the city. So she was rather surprised at herself for feeling reluctant now. You're a miserable coward, she told herself brutally.

However, the lessons were becoming much less nerve-racking, even enjoyable, as Barbara had learned to relax and feel more secure on her horse. She began to find it easier to sit still in the saddle, to give the leg aids without lurching forward, and to rise to the trot without bouncing. Occasionally she had a fleeting sense of the joyful rhythm she knew from somewhere inside that riding was all about. For people like Mrs. Lindsay, riding's like that all the time, she thought, and although this encouraged her, she still did not manage to canter.

"I must have a psychological block about cantering," she told Miss Brown after a lesson in which she had failed yet again to get Polka to canter.

"Psychological block, my foot," snorted Miss Brown. "Perseverence is what you want."

"I am trying," said Barbara, feeling hurt. You don't know what it's like to feel afraid, she thought, as she led Polka into the stable.

"Well, keep on trying, isn't it," said Miss Brown, twinkling gently at her. "Ah, don't worry, Barbara, I'll have you cantering by New Year. See if I don't."

"Isn't Miss Brown relentless," said Barbara to Peggy later. "No wonder your mother won an Olympic medal."

One afternoon after Sybille's lesson, Miss Brown allowed Barbara to try the sidesaddle on Gwydion. It certainly felt different—perhaps safer?—Barbara could not decide. It was not particularly comfortable. The seat of the saddle was too large for Barbara so that she had to sit well forward to tuck her knees round the pommels, and this made it even more difficult to sit up straight and not slip round sideways to the left. She felt very high up and Gwydion's head seemed very far away at the end of the rein. She did not feel that she would have much control if he decided to gallop off or otherwise take advantage of his unwary rider. At the end of half an hour she had to admit regretfully that sidesaddle was not the answer for her after all. There was nothing for it but to listen to Miss Brown and keep trying to master cantering in the ordinary way. Perhaps I'll try sidesaddle again when I'm older, she said to herself.

That Christmas was one of the most enjoyable Barbara and her parents had ever known. People were constantly dropping in at Mount Severn to chat and drink damson gin prepared according to Sybille's recipe. There were picnics in the stable for school friends who came for a ride and got roped in afterwards to help with the tack-cleaning. There were a great many parties and dances and all the parents were often out until very late. Both families joined a large crowd that accompanied the Silver Band on its carol-singing tour of the town on Christmas Eve, and made frequent stops at the various pubs to sing to the customers and have a drink themselves. People waved and smiled at them, and even Barbara's mother had to admit that she felt at home among these small town people.

Barbara worked doggedly at her story through all these pleasant distractions. On the day before New Year's Eve the neat copy of "The Blind Pony" was finished. She had made a considerable number of changes and now the story filled three substantial exercise books. She felt a sense of achievement and took it downstairs to show her parents.

"It's very neat," said her father. "That's quite an effort you've made there, Barbara."

"You've certainly stuck to it," agreed her mother. "It'd be nice to read it some time. But I daresay you want to let your friends read it first," she added tactfully.

Barbara had not told her parents that she intended to send the book to a publisher. She said, "Oh yes, lots of people want to read it. You can read it after, Mother, if you promise not to laugh at it for being a horse book."

Her parents exchanged amused glances. "All right, I promise," her mother smiled. She had been in a good mood since Christmas, thought Barbara. She seemed to have had a change of heart about horses, too. Barbara still could not get over her surprise at her Christmas presents, a lovely brown tweed hacking jacket *and* a pair of jodhpur boots. They were the first horsy presents her parents had ever given her.

Barbara had gone to the County Library and made a careful list of the publishers who seemed to do mostly horse stories. One of the librarians found their correct addresses for her. She chose the publisher of her favorite series and wrote a letter to send with the manuscript.

Dear Sir,
    I have written this horse story called "The Blind Pony."
It is about a hundred pages long. I don't know if it is any
good or not. I am sorry that it is not typed but I do not
have a typewriter. I hope you can read my writing. I am
thirteen years old.

                                          Yours faithfully,
                                          Barbara Dawes

After showing the letter to Peggy and receiving her ap-
proval, she wrapped the parcel well with string and sticky
tape saved from Christmas. Peggy accompanied her to
the Post Office. Barbara felt awed and excited as the as-
sistant drew blue lines on the parcel and put it on one
side. My first book off to the publisher, she thought.
    "Your first book off to the publisher," said Peggy. "We
must celebrate. Let's go and have some coffee at Morgan's Cafe. I'll treat you. We'll have some buns too."
    "Oh, great, thanks," said Barbara absently. She won-
dered how long it would be before she heard anything
from the publisher. A month? Three months? And what
would they say? Perhaps by some miracle they would like
it and even want to publish it. Barbara had read about
people who had books published when they were not
much older than she was. She envisioned herself rushing
into the kitchen to show her parents a letter from the
publisher accepting her book, and telling everyone about
it in the *County Times*. But it was silly to expect the publisher to think that her story was that good. They'd be
more likely to think that it was very unoriginal and badly
written.
    "Promise not to tell anyone I've sent it to a publisher,"
she said urgently to Peggy as they waited for their coffee
and buns in Morgan's. "I couldn't bear anyone to laugh

at me. And please don't remind Tessa and Ian, they'll only ask me about it in front of someone."

"All right, if you don't want me to," said Peggy, giggling. "But I do think you're funny. I'd want to tell everybody if it was me." She stirred several spoonfuls of sugar into her coffee and tasted it.

"But what if it's no good and I get a nasty letter telling me not to be a silly girl and to concentrate on my school work?" Barbara picked the currants out of her bun and nibbled at them. "Perhaps I shouldn't have sent it, it's no good really."

"Oh, you're crazy," cried Peggy in exasperation. "What does it matter what they say? You've got to believe in yourself and stop telling everybody how hopeless you are." Peggy sipped her coffee. "You ought to be thinking about what story you're going to write next. I hope you've got lots of ideas."

"Well, a few," said Barbara evasively.

CHAPTER EIGHT

A Riding Lesson

ON THE MORNING of New Year's Eve Barbara had booked a riding lesson. The night before Mrs. Lindsay had stopped by unexpectedly to tell Barbara that she could ride Gwydion tomorrow, and instead of going in the ordinary class, Barbara could accompany her on Coningsby on a ride up to the Bryn Bank.

Barbara was thrilled but rather alarmed by the privilege of riding with Peggy's mother. She was ready far too early, dressed in her new riding clothes. A sharp wind had blown up and both horses were restless, tossing their heads and swishing their tails. Knowing Gwydion's unpredictability, Barbara began to feel uneasy but Mrs. Lindsay merely said, "They've got the wind under their tails today. Put Gwydion's bridle on, Barbara."

By the time Barbara had bridled Gwydion, Mrs. Lindsay was already in the saddle, sitting quite calmly as Coningsby circled and shook his head. Barbara scrambled on to Gwydion from the mounting block. He did not feel like standing still today but somehow she arrived in the saddle. Mrs. Lindsay watched patiently while Barbara shortened her stirrup leathers, fiddling clumsily with the buckles as Gwydion moved restlessly about.

"Good," said Mrs. Lindsay. "Don't worry, he won't run away with you, he's too lazy. He's only showing off a bit so as not to lose face with Consy." Mrs. Lindsay gave Barbara an encouraging smile. "Are you ready? Good. Off we go now." She rode ahead, and Barbara was filled with her usual envy at the way Mrs. Lindsay looked as she sat on her fine old horse. She was wearing an old navy blue fisherman's sweater and jeans and, sitting casually in the saddle, she turned now and then to look critically at Barbara and tell her to sit up straight and push her heels down.

They rode up Fron Lane which wound slowly to the top of the Bryn Bank between bare hawthorn hedges. At the top they looked at the wintry view across the town to the hills of Kerry and Mochdre, ochre and brown under the pale sun. "Who'd want to live anywhere else?" said Mrs. Lindsay with a pleased sigh.

The wind was cold but not strong on the bare hill and they trotted sedately along the bridle path, ignored by the grazing sheep. After ten minutes the path became steeper, and Mrs. Lindsay called, "Sitting trot now, and push him on and make him canter."

Barbara caught her breath, but Coningsby was already cantering ahead, taking Mrs. Lindsay out of earshot, so there was nothing for it but to do as she was told. However, Gwydion gave her no opportunity to hang back; he did not like being left behind. He broke into a determined canter before Barbara could shorten the reins, and she snatched at his mane to keep from slipping forward over his shoulder. Somehow she managed to push herself back into the saddle and sort out the reins. After sliding about for a few moments she suddenly found her balance and sat more securely. I'm cantering, she thought incredulously. I'm really cantering.

"Well done!" Mrs. Lindsay called. "Now use your legs. Keep him going, don't let him slow down!" Gwydion had no intention of slowing down. For several moments Barbara cantered joyfully, the nearest she had ever been to experiencing in reality the feeling she could always imagine so vividly, of flying along on the back of a horse, set free from the clumsy constraints of her overweight body.

Nancy drew Coningsby back alongside Gwydion and both horses slowed down. Barbara jolted in the saddle as Gwydion slowed to a jog-trot but she hardly noticed. Mrs. Lindsay smiled at the brimming elation on Barbara's face.

"There, that wasn't so bad, was it?"

"It was wonderful," said Barbara. "I cantered. I really cantered! Oh gosh, my legs feel all weak." She was taking in great gasps of air, grinning idiotically and patting Gwydion. "But he took off with me really," she added truthfully. "I didn't really tell him to canter."

"All it takes is practice," said Mrs. Lindsay. "Perseverance, as Miss Brown would say. Come on, we'll trot as far as the road and then walk back, it's downhill all the way."

As they rode home side by side Barbara could not stop repeating to herself, I cantered, I really cantered! She only half listened to Mrs. Lindsay chatting about Coningsby's twenty-ninth birthday. "I always get the vet to have a look at him on his birthday, to make sure he's still sound in heart and wind. I want him to have a look at Bianca too, while he's here."

"But there's nothing wrong with her, is there?" said Barbara, coming back to earth in alarm.

"No, I just want him to look at—" Suddenly a sheep bounded across their path. Coningsby reared backwards and Gwydion shied off sideways down the hill.

Barbara was thrown forward onto Gwydion's neck, losing her stirrups. She felt herself sliding over his shoulder as he made eagerly for home. She thought, Oh please, not again! when the command, "Sit up!" clicked in her brain. She found she had grasped Gwydion's thick mane with both hands. As he began to slow down from a canter to a trot she pushed herself slowly back into the saddle. She moved one hand from his mane to the pommel of the saddle and lurched upright.

All Miss Brown's pupils practiced trotting without stirrups and this stood Barbara in good stead now. Gwydion jogged determinedly down the path, tossing his head, as Barbara sat stirrupless in the saddle, still clinging to the pommel with her left hand, trying to catch up the reins with her right. She was suddenly determined to stop him properly—when she wanted him to stop, not when he felt like it. When she finally had the reins in both hands again, she cautiously let go the anchoring pommel. Gwydion's ears were poised; he seemed to sense her release of tension and began to slow into a walk. Barbara gritted her teeth and used her legs until she had forced him into an unwilling jog for a further few paces, and then gave the aids to stop. Gwydion slouched to a halt that would have horrified Miss Brown, but Barbara felt that her honor had been satisfied.

Then the realization hit her. *I didn't fall off!* She almost shouted the words. She turned to see Mrs. Lindsay riding up, looking delighted. "Good girl!" she said. "You really kept your head there!"

"I didn't fall off," said Barbara, giggling weakly.

Mrs. Lindsay dismounted and put Barbara's feet back

into the stirrup irons. "You certainly got the better of Gwydion," she said, looking up with a smile.

"I remembered about sitting up just in time," said Barbara.

"You did jolly well," said Mrs. Lindsay. "Lots of people would have fallen right off."

And I cantered, remembered Barbara joyfully. I cantered, and then I got run away with and I didn't fall off.

"You wait till we tell Miss Brown," Mrs. Lindsay said as she mounted. "She'll be so pleased."

Basking in the congratulations of Mrs. Lindsay and Miss Brown, Barbara went happily indoors for lunch. She told her parents about cantering as they ate toad-in-the-hole. They seemed very pleased, and much more interested than usual.

"I nearly fell off, actually," Barbara told them airily. "A sheep jumped up in front of us and the horses shied. But I managed to stick on. Gwydion was amazed!"

"You be careful," said her father. "Mind you don't get hurt. Horses are big, dangerous animals if you ask me."

"But I didn't fall off, Dad really! Mrs. Lindsay says I kept my balance really well. Mind you I expect I will fall off again, sometimes, but everyone falls off." Barbara took a gulp of milk. "But, as long as you wear your crash cap, that's the main thing."

"It takes seven falls to make a rider," said her mother. "Isn't that what they say?"

"Yes," said Barbara in surprise. "How did you know that?"

"Well, one can't live in a place like Mount Severn without picking up some of the horsy idiom. Mainly from Tessa, I should think, telling me all about how she's going to be an Olympic medallist at the age of fourteen."

"She does go on," said Barbara, helping herself to an-

other spoonful of greens from the vegetable dish. "She
drives everyone crazy."

"Yes. At least this isn't the kind of horsy establishment
that encourages people to think like that, and it could be,
Nancy Lindsay being who she is."

Barbara could hardly believe her ears. Had her parents
had a change of heart towards the horsy question, as she
called it? And the riding kit at Christmas too, she
thought, it was too good to be true. She could not con-
ceive of grownups changing what seemed to be funda-
mental attitudes without some very good reason. She
eyed her mother suspiciously.

"We've got plenty of milk today," her mother was saying. "Shall I make some coffee for us? 'Through milk,' as
Miss Brown would say." She stood up and started stack-
ing the dishes. "Let's be posh and have it in the living
room." She sounded suddenly nervous and glanced at
Barbara's father as though for reassurance.

"Good idea." Barbara's father rose from the table. "I'll
get the tray. You get the cups and saucers, Barbara."

The sudden tension put Barbara on her guard. Maybe
they found a house, she thought. She helped her father
carry the dishes and took a chair next to him.

For a few silent minutes, they all sat self-consciously in
the living room sipping the thick milky coffee.

"I must say, we all seem to be adjusting very well here,"
her mother began. "You're happy at school, aren't you,
Barbara, and you've made friends with Peggy." Barbara
shifted in her chair.

"Your mother and I have been saying how pleased we
are to see that you're doing so well, especially at the stables," said her father tentatively. He set his cup down.
"Miss Brown says what a help you are and how good you
are with the horses."

Barbara eyed her parents. "You've found a house," she said weakly.

"Oh, no," her mother replied quickly. "The house situation is hopeless. There's nothing on the market at all. We'll probably be staying here for quite a bit yet."

"Oh good," said Barbara, relaxing. "I like it here. I'd like to stay here forever."

"Hm, I don't know about that," said her father, picking up his cup again. "But even when we do get a house we aren't likely to move very far away. You'd still be able to come to the stables to ride."

Barbara said nothing.

"What we're trying to say," said her mother, leaning forward in sudden determination, "is that we're very pleased that you've settled down and we're pleased to see that being round the horses hasn't turned you into too much of a horse fanatic. Another thing, you used to have such impossible daydreams." She took a deep breath and glanced at her husband. "I worried that you were running away from reality. Well, you've come out of your shell a great deal and that's really good, but you know that there's still one thing we worry about."

Barbara put down her coffee and began to get up. Her father laid his hand on her shoulder and pulled her down again. "Barbara, I want you to listen to your mother."

"Do calm down, Barbara," said her mother quietly. "I haven't even begun yet and you're on the defensive. Now just listen to me and don't get angry." She reached for Barbara's hand, but Barbara jerked away. "I know you think I'm always nagging you but I don't know what else I can do. You worry me so much and you don't do anything to help yourself." Her mother looked at her husband helplessly. "We've just got to tackle this weight problem of yours, Barbara. You can't run away from it forever."

No, thought Barbara. No. No. The palms of her hands began to sweat and she wiped them down her sweater.

"You must lose at least thirty pounds," her mother was saying. "And it's not because I want you to look slim because it's fashionable, I couldn't care less about that."

Oh, sure, thought Barbara bitterly. She stared over her mother's shoulder, trying to detach herself from the scene, to switch herself off until it was over.

"It's your health I'm concerned about," her mother raised her voice. "I don't want you to spend your life battling with blood pressure and diabetes and goodness knows what else."

Barbara stared into space. She had been right about everything being too good to be true. She should have known there was something fishy about that riding kit as well. All her parents had been doing was buttering her up. And now the dreary battle was going to start all over again.

Her mother continued as calmly as she could, "I just don't believe that you don't mind being thirty pounds overweight," she said. "Why can't you swallow your pride and admit it? Then we could all tackle the problem together. We know it won't be easy, Barbara. We know it's a big thing to deal with. That's why your father and I are so anxious to help you."

"I don't mind being fat," interrupted Barbara. "As far as I'm concerned it's irrelevant. I'm going to be a writer and writers don't have to be thin. Sybille says when I'm writing best-sellers it won't matter if I'm two hundred pounds, so there," she panted.

"She would!" said her mother angrily. "I might have known you'd have been talking to her. Wait till I see her."

"She's the only person I've ever met who's shown any understanding of what it's like to be nagged and persecuted about dieting. She went through hell to be what she wanted to be in spite of everyone," Barbara choked, "and if she can so can I."

"She's got a chip on her shoulder," snapped her mother.

"She hasn't, she—"

"Stop it, Barbara." Her father's voice broke through. "Let me tell her, Joan," he said, taking Barbara's hand in his. "Listen to me," he said calmly. "What we were going to suggest was, since your riding is coming along so well—"

"It's not, I've only cantered once and I'm always falling off."

"Well, Mrs. Lindsay says you've got the makings of a good rider," her father went on firmly. "She tells me that if you were really slim and fit you could be pretty good. Besides, I thought you were over the moon today because you didn't fall off."

Barbara felt betrayed. So that was why Mrs. Lindsay had taken her out on Gwydion. She might have known that she had been plotting with her parents. But at the same time, Barbara was aware of the contrariness of her reaction. She *did* want to ride, didn't she? And she was pleased that Mrs. Lindsay thought she might make a good rider, wasn't she? But Mrs. Lindsay was probably only saying that, Barbara concluded. She didn't really mean it, she just wanted to get in with Barbara's parents. Barbara pulled her hand away from her father's.

"What we decided, your mother and I," said her father, choosing his words carefully, "was that if you really made an effort to slim down," he looked Barbara in the eye— "and we'd all help you, not just us but the Lindsays too, and we'd have a quiet word at school as well so that you could take packed lunches instead of having school dinner—" he took a quick breath and glanced at his wife, "If we really had a go at it, what we thought was, as soon as you lost your thirty pounds we could start looking out for a horse for you."

"Yes," her mother rushed on, "and now that I'm working as well and we've no mortgage round our necks we aren't badly off." She looked at Barbara hopefully. "We might be able to afford a really good horse, Barbara. We could get Mrs. Lindsay and Miss Brown to help us look." Her mother sat on the edge of her seat.

Barbara swallowed. This was the last incentive she had ever expected her parents to offer her. A horse. The one thing she had always wanted more than anything else.

"I don't want any bribes." She heard her own voice, cold and very far away. "I don't want any pony except Bianca anyway," she paused nervously, and then rushed on. "I'm not bothered about being fat. It doesn't stop me from doing what I want to do—not even from riding," she added triumphantly. "People have just got to learn to accept me as I am. If I ever feel like going on a diet I will, but it'll be when *I* decide." She looked at her mother calmly. "You can nag and scream at me until you're blue in the face, but it won't make me diet if I don't want to. And you needn't think I'm going to let myself be psychoanalyzed by Gwyn Edwards, either," she added, her old grievance flaring up, "And I don't want any pony except—"

"You ungrateful little beast!" her mother jumped up in tears. "I wash my hands of you. Why did I ever think I'd enjoy having a daughter?" she wailed and slammed out of the room.

Barbara stared after her, horrified, angry and guilty all at once.

"Well, I hope you're satisfied," said her father, slowly rising. "Now get up to your room and stay there until you can apologize to your mother. And just ask yourself if you aren't cutting off your nose to spite your face."

The tone of her usually easy-going father's voice frightened Barbara. She rushed out to the stables, flung her arms round Bianca's neck and sobbed hopelessly.

CHAPTER NINE

On the Bryn Bank

BARBARA did not cry for long. There seemed to be no point. She felt restless and unable to think. In a book she would have saddled her pony and gone for a good gallop, she thought irritably. "I wish I could ride off on you, Bianca," she told the pony moodily.

"Why don't you take her for a little walk?"

Barbara jumped, and turned to see Miss Brown smiling kindly at her. She felt conscious of her red eyes; Miss Brown was bound to notice that she had been crying.

"I hope you're not going to forget her, now you're cantering."

"Oh no, no!" She could not say, I only want to learn to ride so I can ride Bianca; it would sound so presumptuous.

"She'd like a little exercise," Miss Brown smiled, coming closer, "and it would be good schooling for her if you took her out for a while. You could go along the river path. Bit of fresh air, do you both good."

"Oh!" said Barbara, stroking Bianca's nose, "Would it be all right? I'd love to."

"Off you go, then. Clip a rein to her headcollar." Miss Brown gestured Barbara toward the tack room. "She'll be as good as gold. She likes you."

"Do you really think so? Thank you very much." Barbara hurried to fetch a leading rein.

Barbara decided against taking the easy river path, where Tessa and Ian were likely to be playing. They would be sure to badger her with questions about where she was taking Bianca and why she had been crying. She set off slowly up Fron Lane to the Bryn Bank. Bianca came along willingly, delighted to be out, and peered around and snorted at the winter hedges. She walked out well, arching her neck and carrying her tail gaily. She'd grown up in the past few months, Barbara noticed, and was developing into a beautiful horse, although rather shaggy at the moment in her winter coat. As if there could be any pony but her, thought Barbara.

Barbara began to find walking up the steep lane rather hard going. She grew hot and had to stop for frequent rests. Bianca waited patiently, looking at her curiously, and Barbara felt ashamed, as though she was letting Bianca down. She plodded grimly alongside Bianca, her breath coming in shorter and shorter bursts and her heart pounding. At last they reached the path which led to the top of the Bryn Bank where she had cantered on Gwydion that morning, and she stopped thankfully to rest. At length her pulse slowed down and she set off once more, striding cheerfully. This path was not so steep and the going was easier.

It was cold and windy on the hill, clear and exhilarating; Bianca danced a little as her mane and tail lifted in the wind. In a sudden impulse Barbara pulled the bands from her braids and shook her hair loose, and even ran a little way with Bianca trotting beside her. The winter sun was already beginning to set, lighting the sky and the countryside with long crimson shafts, glinting through her hair as it blew about her face.

Barbara was suddenly, deeply stirred by the beauty of the landscape, the sharpness of the air, the grace of the white pony by her side. The memory of the struggle to climb the steep hill, the sense of shame and disgust at the comparison between Bianca's beauty and her own obese clumsiness and racing pulse, fell from her like broken chains. Here on the hill she was as free and as light as air, her burdens forgotten in the valley below. This is what it would be like if I lost weight, she thought emotionally.

She tossed her hair back lightly. The gesture reminded her of Sybille, and of their conversation.

But what about being a writer, she asked herself, and not caring about what people think? She thought of Sybille, huge and splendid in her sidesaddle costume, utterly herself from her massed dark hair to her buttoned boots.

"But I'm not Sybille," Barbara said to Bianca, who pricked her ears and nodded at the sound of Barbara's voice. "I couldn't be like that, I'd just look ridiculous." She pressed her lips resolutely together.

Barbara and Bianca walked and jogged along the hilltop path for a long way before turning for home. Barbara was thinking, Oh God I've got to do it. Oh God it's going to be awful. "And the worst thing will be everyone giving me advice," she told Bianca.

It was dark when they arrived back at the Mount Severn stables. Barbara's mood began to fall to pieces at the prospect of apologizing to her mother. She did not intend to mention her hilltop decision; she could not face any discussion of what kind of diet to go on and how everyone would rally round to give moral support.

The sound of Bianca's hooves brought Miss Brown out of the long stable, a bucket of feed in her hand. "That was a long walk," she smiled at Barbara. "Haven't you been out in the wind, both of you!" She patted Bianca's nose affectionately.

"It was lovely," said Barbara, smiling tiredly and handing over the leading rein. "I feel so much better. There was a wonderful sunset."

"The more she goes out, the better now." Miss Brown led Bianca into the stables. "We'll have to take her out on the roads too, to get her used to traffic, if we're going to break her in."

"Break her in!" said Barbara. "Are you really going to?"

"Well, we'll see how things go," said Miss Brown vaguely. "The vet's coming tomorrow," she added. "He always comes on New Year's Day to look at Consy. We thought he could look at Bianca while he's here, to check her eyes for one thing."

"It'll be awfully sad if she can never really see properly," said Barbara, unbuckling Bianca's headcollar. "She'll be so beautiful when she's fully grown. I was thinking this afternoon what she'll look like when she loses her winter coat." She paused a minute and continued tentatively, "Miss Brown, I hope I'll be able to help if you do decide to break her in."

"Why yes, aren't you the obvious person?"

"Oh! Am I? But don't you think I'm too fat?"

Miss Brown said kindly, "Oh, that's only puppy fat, you'll soon trim down if you go for plenty of walks. And less chips, isn't it?"

If only it was as easy as that, thought Barbara. But she

felt a burst of confidence that Miss Brown seemed to take for granted that she would help with Bianca's training. Perhaps this was a turning point in her life. "I could get slim for you, Bianca," she whispered to the pony, "even if your eyes never get better."

After a while Barbara plucked up her courage and went nervously indoors to face her mother. She was thoroughly taken aback to find her mother and Mrs. Lindsay in a very good mood, telephoning all their friends to invite them round for a New Year's Eve party. "They've had a few drinks," Peggy told her in an awed voice. "My Dad and your Dad have gone off in a huff."

"Crumbs," said Barbara. "Where are Ian and Tessa?"

"Watching telly. They've made themselves jam sandwiches and lemonade. Come on, we'll do ourselves some scrambled eggs on toast."

In the kitchen Peggy cut slices of bread while Barbara whisked eggs in a bowl.

"Only one slice of toast for me," she told Peggy.

Peggy's eyebrows shot up. "Oh?! New Year's resolution?"

"Ugh, don't say that." Barbara paused in her mixing. "It is sort of though, I suppose. But don't you dare mention it to anyone. You know what people are like, they can't wait to start talking about the latest diets and giving you advice. And if I ever see *you* giving me warning looks when there's shortbread on the table I'll throw the plate at you."

Barbara's parents were short-tempered at breakfast next morning. They drank black coffee and snapped at Barbara. Annoyed, she changed her mind about apologizing and defiantly ate two pieces of toast thickly spread with butter and jam, and put sugar in her coffee instead of saccharine. It was not until too late that she remembered the decision she had made yesterday. I don't care, she thought, I'm going to be a writer anyway. Then she thought, No! I'm really going to try this time. I'll make a proper start tomorrow.

"And where do you think you're going in such a hurry?" asked her father as she quickly rinsed her dishes under the hot tap and left them to drain.

"Mrs. Lindsay said I could have another riding lesson today at ten o'clock," said Barbara. "I must go and help to catch the horses."

"You'll do nothing of the sort," said her father. "If you think you're going riding after the disgraceful way you spoke to your mother and me yesterday you can think again. I haven't heard you give us a proper apology yet, either."

"I haven't had the chance," Barbara retorted. "You were both drunk yesterday."

"Well, that settles it," said her father. "You can just go and tell Mrs. Lindsay that you're not riding today, that you're cleaning your room."

Barbara looked at her mother who avoided her eye. She stamped off down to the stable where Mrs. Lindsay was grooming Coningsby.

"My mother says I can't ride today, I've got to clean my room," Barbara told her.

Mrs. Lindsay looked up casually. "Right-o. Another time, perhaps," she said briefly, and returned to her grooming. Barbara felt rebuffed. She wondered if her mother had told Mrs. Lindsay about their row yesterday. They had seemed to be getting friendlier lately. She might have known Mrs. Lindsay would support her parents. Sybille was obviously the only adult who would ever really be on her side.

Barbara cleaned her room until she heard her parents go out. Then she took some of her remaining Christmas money and hurried to the corner shop on the Crescent where she bought a package of chocolate biscuits and a Mars Bar. Back at home, she put on the electric fireplace in her bedroom, made herself a cup of sweet coffee and settled down with one of Mrs. Lindsay's old horse books and her supply of food. One last treat, she told herself.

She had to hide the food quickly when Peggy came rushing in to announce that the vet had arrived.

"I can't come out today. I had a row with my mother. I've got to stay in my room," said Barbara, exaggerating the truth with a martyred expression.

"Oh, how rotten," Peggy made a face. "Oh, come down, they won't know."

"I'll be in awful trouble if they come back and find me with the horses. They'd like an excuse to stop me riding altogether," Barbara added, sitting upon her bed. "But you'll report back to me what the vet says about Bianca, won't you?"

"Yes, I'll come up as soon as I know. But what on earth have you done?"

"Oh, it was another row about dieting. I said I couldn't be bothered."

Peggy looked at her in amazement. "But what about your New Year's resolution?"

"It's *my* resolution, it's got nothing to do with them."

"Oh." Peggy went downstairs rather mystified.

Barbara returned half-heartedly to her biscuits and her book, both of which seemed boring and stale. She was annoyed and fed up with herself. It had been so silly to tell Peggy that tale about her parents confining her to her room. Now she would miss hearing what the vet had to say about Bianca. I don't care, she told herself perversely. I'll never be able to ride her anyway. I can always take her for walks if I want to. I don't need to be slim for that, and Bianca doesn't have to have fantastic eyesight either. What I ought to be doing is thinking what my next story is going to be about.

At lunchtime her parents were in a better mood. Barbara apologized to her mother for being rude the day before and at breakfast time.

"I accept your apology. I'd like to see it backed up by a more cooperative attitude." Barbara's mother said stiffly. Barbara sensed that her mother felt sorry too, but she hurried off to hear the news about Bianca. She found Peggy and they went down to the stable together.

"The vet said he couldn't really tell us anything we didn't know already," Peggy told her as they leaned in their usual place on Bianca's partition. The white pony was pleased to see them and leaned sociably over to be rubbed behind her furry ears, "He said her eyesight's improved quite a bit since she was a foal," Peggy went on, "but he didn't know whether it would get any better—it would always be likely to be worse in bright light, for instance. And it wouldn't make any difference to her breeding prospects. He said if we sent her to a chestnut stallion we might get a palomino foal."

"Did he say anything about breaking her in?"

"He said we should try and see how it went." Peggy eased the tangles out of Bianca's mane with her fingers, glancing sideways at Barbara.

"Mum and Miss Brown are quite keen to break her in," said Peggy. "Bianca's so gentle, she'll be marvellous for nervous people just learning to ride, and she'll be just the right size for lightweight grownups."

"I suppose she will," said Barbara sadly. She thought Bianca far too special to be just a riding school horse. There ought to be a more glorious future for her, one in which Barbara was somehow involved. But the reality was that even if she helped to break Bianca in, Barbara would probably end up being the only person unable to ride her. She would really have to start dieting again tomorrow. If only she could do it her own way, at her own pace, without having to worry about catching her mother's exasperated eye every time the temptation proved too much for her.

Peggy realized the reason for Barbara's silence and said, "Oh dear, I'm sorry. That wasn't very tactful of me."

"That's all right," said Barbara, still scratching between Bianca's ears. "You didn't say anything that wasn't true."

"But you've made your resolution, don't forget. You'll soon get thin if you stick to it, you'll see."

Barbara smiled weakly. "I keep trying to tell myself it doesn't really matter." She faced Peggy. "Like Sybille says, you don't have to be thin to be a writer or go to college. But then I think about Bianca, and riding in general, and seeing how marvellous your mother looks on Consy, and then it *does* matter, and I want to get slim really desperately." Barbara looked down, suddenly embarrassed.

"You'll do it, Barbara, you really will," said Peggy earnestly. She touched Barbara's arm tentatively. "I think you deserve to be a good rider and have a nice horse. You really care about horses, much more than I do really."

Barbara sighed, leaning over the partition and gazing

at the straw. "The trouble is I get so terribly, terribly hungry. And when I'm hungry I just forget about everything
except getting something to eat. I just can't seem to stop
myself." She shrugged.

"It must be rotten," Peggy sympathized. "I get hungry
of course, but not all the time. Mind you I think I eat
quite a lot. But I'm lucky, it doesn't make me fat."

Peggy's remarks cheered Barbara a little although, she
told herself, sympathy from a thin person didn't mean
much. If I didn't know Sybille felt the same, she thought,
I really would wonder if I was a bit mental.

Her mother was slightly less brusque at teatime although she set out crispbreads instead of bread and butter for Barbara, and fruit yogurt instead of cake. Her
father read the paper. The atmosphere was slightly
strained. No one mentioned horses or dieting, or New
Year's resolutions. Barbara went to her room as soon as
she could, back to her book and the few remaining biscuits.

That evening it began to snow, and it continued for
several days. There was no riding; all the horses were
brought into the long stable at night and turned out during the day to exercise themselves. Coningsby and Bianca
were privileged and stayed in all the time except for short
walks on a straw path laid round the yard.

The roads were too slushy for Barbara to take Bianca
for walks so she stayed in her room moodily reading or
chatting to Peggy or trying not very successfully to think
of a new story. Inside, she fought a constant struggle
about whether to diet or not. She would wake up each
morning feeling cheerful and optimistic and would eat a
frugal breakfast, but by eleven o'clock she would give in
helplessly to the overwhelming urge to steal some biscuits

or a bowl of cereal from the larder or to buy chocolate from the local shop. The rest of the day Barbara would be in a rage and then console herself that it did not matter anyway because she was going to be a writer. The day would end up with promises to make a fresh start the next morning, when the ritual would begin all over again.

By the last day of the holidays Barbara was in despair, touchy with everyone at Mount Severn and then overly apologetic, much to their exasperation. I really am going mental, she told herself, looking out of the living room window at the snowy lawn and the streaky brown and white countryside. Peggy must think I am the original hopeless fat girl now.

Peggy came looking for her just then, dressed in her thick brown jacket and boots. "Let's go and take Bianca for a walk," she said. "Miss Brown says it's okay, and the roads have cleared a bit. Mum's taking Consy out."

"That's a good idea," said Barbara thankfully. She hurried into her winter clothes and followed Peggy down to the stables. Bianca was alone and whinnied when they joined her. "She knows she's going out. Look at her, she practically puts her headcollar on herself," said Peggy, fastening the buckles and clipping on the lead rein.

They led her into the yard which had been swept clear of snow but was wet and muddy. Gwyn Edwards was standing by the back door, peering hopefully inside. Barbara's heart sank. That's all I need, she thought.

"Oh, hello, Mr. Edwards, there's nobody in except us," Peggy called out.

Gwyn Edwards came towards them, smiling inside his beard. He was rubbing his hands together. "Whew, it's cold," he said.

"Mum's out riding Consy and Miss Brown's just gone

to Shrewsbury," Peggy told him. "And Dad and Barbara's parents are down at school."

"And we're taking Bianca out," said Barbara hastily.

Gwyn Edwards looked embarrassed. "I see, well, I really wanted to see Barbara as it happens. But if you're going out . . ."

"Yes, we are," said Barbara, looking hard at Peggy and hoping that she had got the hint to back her up.

"And Barbara doesn't want to talk to you anyway," said Peggy. "She isn't mad and she's fed up with people nagging her about dieting." She looked at Barbara who had turned scarlet. "Well, you might as well tell him straight," she said.

Gwyn Edwards turned to Barbara, "Your mother worries herself to death about your weight problem you know. She asked me if I could help. This eating business is a funny thing, Barbara. If you could tell me how you feel about it I might be able to make a few suggestions."

Barbara glanced about and took a deep breath. "I get plenty of advice and suggestions, thank you. All of them come from people who can't possibly know what they're talking about. My weight is my problem and nobody else's, and what I choose to do about it is my affair. I don't want to be psychoanalyzed, Mr. Edwards, I just want to be left alone." She tried to speak calmly. Her hands were sweating on the webbing lead rein.

Gwyn Edwards listened, nodding slowly. "I can understand your feeling that way. But I don't go in for psychoanalysis, you know. I'm not a head-shrinker." He tried to sound humorous. Barbara scowled at him. "Don't look at me like that, Barbara," he said quickly. "Oh Lord, I can see I've put my foot in it. But look, if you ever *do* want to have a chat, give me a ring at the office any time."

"Thank you, but I don't think I'll be bothering you," said Barbara stiffly.

Gwyn Edwards nodded. "Well, see how you feel about it. I'll let you take your pony out now." He smiled at them. "Is this Bianca, Peggy? She's growing into a very pretty pony, isn't she?" He patted her awkwardly before turning to go, the two girls waiting politely. As he turned down the lane Peggy looked at Barbara and saw that she was still scarlet and trembling. "Are you all right?" Peggy said with alarm.

"He'll tell my mother," said Barbara, her voice shaking. "He'll tell her how rude I was. God knows what'll happen now. What am I going to do? Oh God, I can't stand it. I wish I was dead."

"He won't tell them," said Peggy urgently. "He won't, he's not like that. Don't be frightened, Barbara."

"It's all right," said Barbara. "I didn't mean to sound panicky." She straightened up. "Huh! And Sybille said Gwyn Edwards was too tactful to bother me about dieting. You wait till I tell her. Huh! Come on, let's take Bianca for this walk. I need some air."

Peggy looked at her doubtfully. Barbara was still flushed. But she was already leading Bianca out and saying, "A walk will do us all good, Peggy. Let's go up onto the Bryn Bank, it'll be lovely in the snow." She was filled with a longing to be out on the hill again and set off briskly, leading Bianca at a jog-trot, leaving Peggy to catch up.

Peggy clearly did not find Fron Lane such a climb as Barbara did, and walked easily beside Bianca. After her initial spurt, Barbara had to grit her teeth and work hard to keep up. She gave the lead rein to Peggy and clenched her fists and climbed, stumbling occasionally on lumps of packed snow. Her breath began to come rather hoarsely and her heart thudded, but it was suddenly of immense importance to reach the top of the hill without stopping, to keep up with Peggy, to break through the resistance of her constricting body. They climbed more and more slowly, Peggy casting worried glances at Barbara's face which was flushing darker and darker under her light red hair.

As they reached the turning to the hill path they saw Peggy's mother riding Coningsby down towards them, stepping delicately across the hard-packed snow. Peggy halted Bianca and Barbara leaned across the pony's soft white back to rest. She buried her head in her hands to stop her eyes from watering and her heart from pounding. Bianca shifted a little under the weight and Barbara stumbled on a lump of snow. Sickeningly, she felt the ground slip from beneath her and she fell heavily, her fingers clutching helplessly at Bianca. Bianca jumped in alarm and something very hard hit the side of Barbara's head.

CHAPTER TEN

An Unconditional Present

PEGGY WAS TOO frightened even to scream. She looked desperately around for her mother. Mrs. Lindsay had flung herself to the ground and was racing towards them down the slippery path.

"She was walking up the hill," Peggy babbled. "She wouldn't stop to rest. She was all worked up about Gwyn Edwards." Peggy grabbed her mother. "I think Bianca kicked her."

Barbara tried to sit up, her breath coming in short fast chokes. Tears ran down her dark face. She clutched her head in her hands and started to speak.

"Don't talk. Calm down," said Mrs. Lindsay. "You're all right." She bent down by Barbara and smoothed her hair back.

"Oh I'm sorry, I'm so sorry," Barbara sobbed and gasped. "Oh my head hurts."

"Don't talk, love, get your breath. You've got a bit of a bang on your head." She spoke calmly and watched Barbara closely. "Bianca caught you when you fell. Thank

God she isn't shod." Mrs. Lindsay turned around, still
squatting. "Peggy, can you take the horses back home?
And can you spare your jacket for Barbara to sit on?"

"Okay," said Peggy, pulling her jacket off quickly. She
hovered anxiously. "Is she all right?"

"Yes, I think so." Mrs. Lindsay looked up. "She just
needs a rest." She smiled reassuringly. Peggy's face re-
laxed, and she looked around for Coningsby and Bianca.
She caught them trailing reins and started to lead them
away. "Oh, and Peggy," her mother called, still crouching
next to Barbara. "See if you can find somebody with a
car."

Peggy nodded and led Coningsby and Bianca down the
hill. "Sit on this," Mrs. Lindsay said to Barbara. She
spread Peggy's jacket out on the snow. "No point in getting wet through."

Barbara smiled weakly and nodded. Her thundering
pulse was slowing a little but she still felt weepy; her head
ached and her legs were hopelessly weak when she tried
to move. She tried to stand up and staggered, and Mrs.
Lindsay helped her sit down again.

"You've given yourself a bit of a fright," Mrs. Lindsay
said. "You're all shaken up. A bit of concussion too, I
don't doubt." She felt Barbara's forehead and her neck.

"It was so lovely that day last week," said Barbara shak-
ily. "When I, when we got to the top and I got my breath
back. It was so easy after that it felt like flying." She
choked a bit and Mrs. Lindsay wiped her forehead. "It
was like breaking out of a prison and being free," Barbara continued slowly, "like when we cantered that day.
I wanted to have that feeling again." She began to cry.
"I'm sorry, I can't help it."

"Don't worry, cry all you like." Mrs. Lindsay stroked

her hair. "We all do it. Especially when we've come within an inch of doing something we wanted to do very much, and not quite managed it."

"But it was such a silly little thing," said Barbara tearfully.

"No it wasn't, if it was important to you."

Barbara nearly confided, "I've had a confusing time lately," but it sounded so pathetic, as if she was asking for sympathy.

Instead she said, "Do you think you'll have to tell my parents? It was my fault it happened and I don't want to worry them."

"You do that already," said Mrs. Lindsay, but kindly.

"Yes I know," muttered Barbara. "I thought I was getting so much better." She wiped her eyes on her sleeve. "I never have to stop on the stairs now and last time I managed the hill all right, too." She twisted her hands; they were still trembling.

"Perhaps you did, but you didn't slip on the snow and get in the way of Bianca's feet last time." Mrs. Lindsay smiled gently.

Barbara continued as if she had not heard. "I wish I was thinner. I really do," she choked, "but it seems so impossible. I'm hopeless." Mrs. Lindsay found her a handkerchief and she blew her nose. "I decide every day that I'm going to be good and not be greedy but then I feel hungry and I just forget. Sybille says if dieting makes me more miserable than being fat I shouldn't bother with it, but I change my mind about whether it does or not every other minute." She began to cry again. "Oh, I'm sorry, I'm sorry," she sniffed frantically.

Mrs. Lindsay dried Barbara's eyes. "For goodness' sake blow your nose again and stop apologizing," she said cheerfully. "But look here, Barbara, there's no question about your Mum and Dad not being told. We'll have to get the doctor to see you—you've had a bang on the head and you can't be too careful about that." Barbara looked alarmed. Mrs. Lindsay said quickly, "You've had an accident, you haven't committed a crime. Anyone can slip on a lump of snow."

"They won't let me take Bianca out anymore," whispered Barbara.

Mrs. Lindsay looked at her seriously. "That's a very unfair thing to say," she said. "And you know it is. I wish you'd give your poor old Mum a chance."

"But she doesn't understand." Barbara wiped her eyes. "I've tried to diet, I've tried and tried and tried but it's just hopeless."

"Nothing's hopeless ever," said Mrs. Lindsay firmly. "You must believe that, Barbara, or you'll never achieve anything. Mind you," she added, "it isn't deciding to do something big that counts. It's the boring little everyday things you have to do that get the job done. You have to ask yourself every time whether you're going to tackle the fence or refuse it, to add sugar or skip dessert . . ."

Barbara looked up at her.

"But don't turn into a fanatic like I did," Mrs. Lindsay smiled. "And do something else for me? Try to tell your mother how you worry about dieting." Barbara looked away. "Tell her what you said to me just now. You can't expect her to understand how you feel unless you tell her, you know."

"I'll try," whispered Barbara.

"Good girl. Well, that ends the sermon for today," said Mrs. Lindsay, giving Barbara's braid a tug. "I've got no business to keep you here talking, actually, you'll catch a chill." Mrs. Lindsay stood up. "It doesn't look as though Peggy has found anyone to fetch us. How are your legs, do you think you can walk downhill?" Barbara nodded. "Well, then, up you get. Feel okay?"

"Yes, thanks," said Barbara, although her legs still felt weak once she was standing on them again. Mrs. Lindsay grasped her elbow and they walked home slowly. The downhill walk was a strain on Barbara's shaky muscles and she had to rest once or twice, feeling weepy and foolish all over again. As they reached Mount Severn the Daweses and Mr. Lindsay pulled in. Barbara's mother gasped when she saw her. "What's happened?"

"I'm all right, Mother," said Barbara. But she could not stop crying.

The doctor diagnosed a slight concussion and ordered Barbara to rest for a few days, but the next morning she woke up with a temperature and a feverish cold. For nearly a week she lay stickily in bed, dozing and blowing her nose and living on hot lemon juice. Despite the discomfort it was a relief to lie in bed with no responsibilities while her mother fussed around her, changing the sheets and fetching more drinks and pills for Barbara's headache. Her bed was a refuge. She dozed, and blew her nose, and thought about nothing.

Then she began to feel better, well enough to sit up in bed and read and have visitors. Peggy, Ian and Tessa came every day after school with books and magazines and the latest news. They would ask to feel the bump on her head and tell her that Bianca missed her; it was very comforting. At the end of the second week Peggy brought in a large bag of colored wool which Sybille had sent.

"I told her you'd thought of crocheting a bedspread," said Peggy, spreading out samples on Barbara's bed. "Mum found some old balls of wool too. We might as well start making squares, it doesn't look as though we're going to get to do much riding this winter."

There had been more snow during the week. Barbara had gotten out of bed early that morning to look out of the window at the white and silent Bryn Bank, but now it was busy and noisy with children on toboggans.

The two girls crocheted steadily, Barbara in bed, Peggy curled up on the overstuffed chair by the window. Barbara found her brain was working again and told Peggy about her new idea for a story. During the week she had read *National Velvet* yet again and this had triggered her imagination. "Reading about the piebald reminded me of your mother's pony, you know, the skewbald, Sligo," she told Peggy.

"He was a rogue, Miss Brown always says," said Peggy, not looking up from her crocheting. "But Mum was really fanatical about him. I wouldn't go near a pony like that."

"The Rogue Pony," thought Barbara. That would be the ideal title for a book to follow "The White Pony." "But how did he become a rogue in the first place?" she asked. "He must have been cruelly treated. Horses aren't born nasty, are they?"

"Mmm, no, I don't think so," Peggy leaned back in her chair for a moment, dropping her work into her lap. "Actually, I don't know where Mum got Sligo from. She doesn't talk about it much nowadays because Tessa gets so overexcited. Mum's frightened she'll bring home a rogue pony one day."

"I'd love to know where Sligo came from," said Barbara. "It would make a marvellous story, how cruelly he was treated when he was young but how eventually your mother rescued him and cured him and trained him."

"But she never cured him really. He was always bad-tempered. Look how Miss Brown always says she'd have had him put down if she'd had her way." She chose another color and hooked it expertly into her square.

"But at least he got looked after properly. What happened to him in the end?"

"Crumbs, I don't know, just died, I expect. He sounds a horrible horse to me."

"Oh, no," said Barbara. "Can't you see what a good story you could write about him? I must persuade Miss Brown to tell me about him, to get some really authentic details." Barbara went back to her crocheting. "It'll be a real story this time, not just one all about what I'd like to have happen to me."

"Oh, don't worry about your last story, the hint's been taken," said Peggy, collapsing suddenly into incomprehensible giggles.

The next day at lunchtime her mother brought Barbara a soft-boiled egg and fingers of bread and butter. She had taken a babyish delight in having this for most of her meals once she had been able to eat again.

"Perhaps you'd like to get up for a bit this afternoon," suggested her mother. "We've been invited to tea with the Lindsays."

"I still don't feel like eating very much," said Barbara, picking at her food.

"That's not surprising," her mother smiled. "You've hardly eaten a thing for ten days. Your face looks a bit thinner, perhaps you've lost a few pounds." She smiled again wryly. "Well, I suppose it's an ill wind that blows nobody any good, as they say."

Later that afternoon Barbara found herself sitting in an armchair by the fire in Peggy's living room with one of the cats purring on her knee. The room was full of the Lindsays, Barbara's parents, Miss Brown and Sybille, sitting about and chatting. Sybille had dropped by to have a bath, since the water pipes at the cottage had frozen up. Then Phil Williams and Gwyn Edwards arrived within ten minutes of each other, looking a little self-conscious with all the company and even more so with each other. "Both after Sybille!" Peggy whispered joyfully to Barbara. Barbara began to feel sorry that she had been so rude to Gwyn Edwards. He was probably much nicer than she had thought.

"Have some more tea, Barbara," said Mr. Lindsay, pouring. He fetched her more brown bread and butter before resuming his place on the arm of his wife's chair. Barbara watched Mrs. Lindsay smile up at her husband and take his hand fondly. They're really in love, thought Barbara romantically. She looked from Mrs. Lindsay to Sybille who was ignoring her two suitors and holding the floor with a description of her most recent sidesaddle lesson, and what a sergeant major Miss Brown was.

Sybille's all alone, thought Barbara. Perhaps she was a natural loner. Perhaps she wasn't interested in getting married. She wondered which of the two women, Mrs. Lindsay or Sybille, she would be most like when she was their age. She thought about Sybille's weight, and wondered whether she really cared about it or not. Awful to think that one might still be thinking, shall I, shan't I, in fifteen years' time.

Barbara sighed. It seemed a hard prospect. She began to feel sleepy and sipped her hot, sweet, comforting tea. But I must stop taking sugar in my tea and coffee, she thought firmly. And I must have a proper talk with Mother about everything. Barbara tried to think about the best way to approach this, but the comfortable atmosphere in the room was catching. She found herself listening to the others as they chatted about the coming season and the possibility of having the dry rot in the roof seen to. I worry about things too much, Barbara told herself.

"We really ought not to keep putting it off," said Mrs. Lindsay, referring to the roof. "Much as I for one would rather spend any spare cash we've got on a nice young horse."

"A horse would be a much better idea," Tessa piped up from a chair in the corner. "I really do need my own horse now."

"That's the last thing you need, my girl, and the last thing you're going to get," Mrs. Lindsay grinned, trying to sound stern. "Anyway, we'll have Bianca to concentrate on now, won't we Barbara?"

"The white palfrey," said Sybille, passing her teacup to Mr. Lindsay for a refill. "You'll be able to ride her in the pageant in June, Barbara. You'd be just right for Queen Elizabeth the First, with your hair." Sybille smiled at Mr. Lindsay and took her cup. "I can see you now. I'll design a costume for you, I've always wanted to see if I could make a farthingale."

Barbara blushed and grinned from her corner, delighted and relieved that she was still considered to have a special relationship with Bianca. "I'll have to get a bit thinner in that case," she said rashly.

Her mother's eyebrows shot up. "Well! I never thought to hear that from your own lips."

"Oh Lord, Barbara, you've done it now," Sybille laughed. "That's a public commitment, that is."

"Well, if anyone teases or torments me all I shall do is to get fat again."

There was general laughter. Barbara felt lighthearted and apprehensive at the same time. It would be simply murder now if she didn't lose weight, she would never hear the end of it. At least she would be able to say to people, well I told you I wouldn't manage it if people nagged me all the time; but it would still sound as though she was making excuses. Oh help, she thought. Oh please don't let it be too hard.

The Lindsay children had been looking restless and impatient for a while, and now Tessa was whispering to her mother. Barbara heard Mrs. Lindsay say, "Okay, but don't bring her indoors," and the children rushed off, giggling. Peggy made faces at Barbara from the doorway.

The grownups all seemed to be in on the secret too. Barbara realized it had something to do with her and began to blush. "What a blush!" said her father. "Why do redheads always blush the most crimson?"

"You should see my wife," said Mr. Lindsay. "Not as much crimson as puce." Whereupon Mrs. Lindsay blushed too.

There was the sound of hooves in the hall and Peggy appeared in the living room doorway. "Quiet now, quiet everyone," she ordered. "Do stop giggling, back there," she said to Ian and Tessa behind her. "Now then, on behalf of the Lindsays, and the Daweses, and Miss Brown, *and* visitors," she nodded graciously at Sybille, Phil and Gwyn. "Mind, you're not really a visitor, Sybille."

"I'm honored!" said Sybille.

"Get *on* with it, Peggy," whispered Ian furiously from outside the room. But before Peggy could say another word, Tessa appeared, leading Bianca by the headcollar. Bianca had a red ribbon tied in her forelock.

Mrs. Lindsay said, "Honestly, I said *not* indoors," but she was laughing.

"Well, we'd like to give Bianca to Barbara as a get-well present," said Peggy in a rush.

"Oh Barbara, have you turned red! I knew she'd go red," Tessa danced about.

Barbara was speechless, and overcome with shyness as everyone in the room looked at her. She looked at her mother. "But I thought a horse was for only if I got thin," she said. "What if I don't get thin?"

"If you get thin, you can have another pony," said Tessa.

"Bianca is for you now," said Mrs. Lindsay. "We thought it was the only right and proper thing. We aren't making any conditions."

"We had a conference to decide," said Ian. "And we were . . . what did you say we were, Dad?"

"Unanimous." Mr. Lindsay gave Barbara a hug.

"Yes, we were unanimous. We all wanted you to have Bianca. So your story has partly come true."

"Oh, but I didn't mean it to be a hint," cried Barbara, blushing wildly.

Everyone laughed. "Go and look after your horse," said her mother smiling.

Barbara looked round to say thank you but the only eyes she met were Miss Brown's. "Thank you," she whispered. "Oh, thank you, I can hardly believe it."

"You take good care of her now," Miss Brown's eyes twinkled at her.

"Oh, I will, I will." Bianca nuzzled and blew at her and

Barbara hugged the pony's head, stroking the downy hair under her throat.

Barbara glanced over to the sofa where her parents sat. She was surprised to see that there were tears in her mother's eyes and her father was blowing his nose. Barbara felt her own eyes fill with tears. "Thank you," she whispered into Bianca's ear.

Peggy gave a great sigh. "Not a dry eye in the place," she said delightedly, looking round at the grownups who were furtively sniffing and blowing their noses.

A month later Barbara arrived home from school to find a parcel waiting for her. Her first reaction was of disappointment. The publisher did not like her book then. Oh well, she might have known. She took the parcel into the stable to open it, watched by Bianca and Coningsby. There was a letter inside. Perhaps they do like it, but they want me to revise it, she thought hopefully.

"Dear Barbara," the letter said,

> I was very interested to read your story "The Blind Pony". It's a very good effort for someone of your age. However, we already publish a considerable number of stories very similar to yours and I do not think we can use any more.
> I hope you will not be discouraged by this. I am sure you know that many famous authors received many rejection slips before achieving success. Your story shows promise and I have no doubt that you too will be an author one day. My advice to you is this: keep on writing about as many different things as possible. Try to be observant of everything around you. Every good writer tries to write from within herself rather than to copy other stories she has read.
> I would also advise you to read as widely as possible, not only children's books but anything you can lay your hands

on. Every writer has much to learn from reading the great
authors; this does not mean that she has to copy them.

I wish you luck with your writing and I should be very
interested to see any of your future stories.

> Yours Sincerely,
> Helen Roberts,
> Children's Book Editor.

Barbara read the letter several times. Mother would
like that last paragraph, she thought. But it really was a
very encouraging letter, serious and not patronizing at
all. Barbara was filled with optimism. The editor really
thinks I might make a writer, she thought, even though
the story was not very original, which Barbara had known
all along. "But she says I will be an author some day," she
said to Bianca.

Try to write about things that are true and real, the
letter said. The strange thing was that now her story had
partly come true, as Ian had pointed out. Did it come
true because I wrote about it, or would it have happened
anyway? Barbara wondered. But I would have loved
Bianca just as much if I hadn't written a story about her.

Perhaps one day I will write the whole story again, telling what really happened, thought Barbara. But not yet,
not for years. After all, the true story of "The Blind
Pony" was only just beginning, and it would be cheating
to look ahead and guess what would happen, or write
what she hoped would happen. The true story might not
turn out to be as glamorous or as exciting as she had once
imagined, but it just might be more interesting in the
end.

Apollo Memorial Library

DATE

MAR 29

MAR

APR 13 04

AL 4780

4780

AL 7319

JF
Old

AUTHOR

Oldham, Mary

The White Pony

TITLE

DATE DUE | BORROWER'S NAME

JF   Oldham, Mary
Old   The White Pony

APOLLO MEMORIAL LIBRARY
219 N. PENNSYLVANIA AVE.
APOLLO, PA   15613

WITHDRAWN

DEMCO